Sheriff of Starr County

Sheriff of Starr County

Book 5 in the Westward Sagas

David A. Bowles

Published by:
Plum Creek Press, Inc.
P.O. Box 701561
San Antonio, Texas 78270-1561
210-827-4122
info@westwardsagas.com
www.westwardsagas.com

Dedication

Carla Rene Bowles Benson
1964-2020

and

Sandra Gale Bowles
1941-2022

Author's Note

Sheriff of Starr County is the fifth book in the Westward Sagas Series. Like the four books before it, each book stands on its own. It is not necessary to read the books in any certain order. The series will continue to be written and published in chronological order. I invite you to ride along with my family of characters or join us anywhere on the trail. I hope you enjoy the ride wherever you start the read.

Chapter One

Will Smith rode into Davis Landing alone. The journey up the Rio Grande River from Fort Brown had taken most of the day. While Will led his horse and burro to the water trough, a skinny teenaged boy cautiously approached. The boy saw a silver star and the pair of revolvers hanging from Will's waist. "Señor, are you...the *Los Diablo Tejano* I wait for?"

"If you mean Texas Ranger, I'm one of them. Why do you ask?" Will yanked the cinch on the horse's saddle, agitated by the boy's remark. It was something he had endured many times during the war with Mexico.

"I have been sent to help you get settled here in Davis Landing. I hear much about Los Diablo Tejanos from Señor Davis and the paper."

"I prefer to be called a Texas Ranger rather than a devil from Texas." Will was aware the Mexican Press had branded the Texas Rangers "Los Diablo Tejanos," a title the rangers earned for some of their brutal actions in the war with Mexico. Most rangers were *Anglos* born in the United States, who only recently came to Texas. *Tejano* meant a person who was in Texas long before the Anglos came.

"I meant no disrespect, señor. I meant it in a good way. Please forgive me," the boy said.

1

"Who is this Señor Davis?" Will asked, wanting to hear what the boy would say. It was a letter from Davis to United States Senator Sam Houston that brought Will to Davis Landing.

"Señor Davis owns all the land around here on both sides of the Rio Bravo as far as you can see. That is why it is called Davis Landing. Señor Davis is also my uncle by marriage to my mother's sister."

"If you live on this side of the border, you best learn to call it the Rio Grande." Will pointed toward the river. "I look forward to meeting your Uncle Davis. Would you show me where the soldiers keep their horses?"

"I take you, señor. What is your name?"

"My name is William. Friends and family call me Will. What's yours?"

"Domingo de la Garza is my name, Señor Will. I will take you to the stables the soldiers have built for you. If you wish, I can be your stable boy, feeding and brushing your animals twice a day except for Sunday. I go to Church and serve as an altar boy on Sunday. I also can clean and polish your boots and belt."

Will looked at his weather-beaten boots "I would like that, Domingo. How much—?"

"For you, only one silver dollar, the U.S. lady liberty, per week."

"That's four dollars a month, Domingo. Why a lady liberty?"

"Our family has much paper money that is worthless. My uncle says silver will never be worthless." Domingo smiled as he opened the large stable door. "Will, I put your horse in a stall with windows on both sides, to keep him cool. The burros go in the corral."

Fresh wood shavings covered the stable floor. The stables smelled more of new wood than fresh horse dung. There were eight stalls, four on each side, with a saddle rack down the middle.

"This is too nice a place for a horse, Domingo." Will smiled as he placed his saddle on the rack and handed his tack to Domingo.

"Your horse is the first to be in it. My job is to keep it clean. Now I take you to the officers' quarters on the hill."

From the steps of the newly constructed barracks, Will saw why this spot was called Davis Landing. The river made a sharp bend and widened into a deep bowl on the riverbank of Davis's land. The water there was deep enough to accommodate steamships landing soldiers and supplies. They heard a steamer's loud blast and saw blue grey smoke billowing in the distance.

Domingo said, "The officers are coming from Fort Brown. If we hurry, you can have first pick of your sleeping quarters." Domingo opened the door to the barracks, one of only two permanent structures at Fort Ringgold. Enlisted men would be housed in tents of eight bunks each. Mess would be served under a big canopy.

Will placed his carbine, saddlebags, and haversack under the bunk in the first room. He inspected what would be his footlocker. Seeing the army-issued blanket and bedding inside, Will thought, *The Rangers never furnished me anything like this.* He picked up the blanket and sniffed it approvingly.

"Will, let's go meet the officers who will command the fort."

"You go ahead, Domingo. I want to clean up and check out this U.S. Army cot first. I'll have plenty of time to meet them later."

Domingo said, "My Uncle, Clay Davis, will be here to pick

you and the officers up for dinner shortly after retreat is called. I will take care of your horse and burro in the morning."

Will knew who the officers were, even though he had never met them. Colonel Jack Hays, commander of the First Texas Riflemen, had briefed Will on each of the U.S. Army officers in charge of Fort Ringgold. Will carried a letter of introduction from Texas Governor George T. Wood and a postscript from Colonel Hays. Will would present them to Major Joseph H. LaMotte, commander of Fort Ringgold, at the proper moment. This would be LaMotte's first command since being seriously injured at the Battle of Monterrey.

Will stretched out on the bunk and closed his eyes, falling asleep on a new army-issued mattress.

Boots tromping and men hollering orders alerted Will that the officers had arrived. He was fully awake but did not open his eyes. Until he heard someone ask, "Who the hell is the vagabond sleeping in the officers' quarters?"

Will listened as Domingo answered, "His name is Will, a Texas Ranger sent by the governor to keep peace here at Davis Landing."

"How would you, a mere peasant boy, know that?"

"I work for Mr. Clay Davis, and he told me! I take care of Señor Will and his animals and I can take care of yours, if you like."

"We have privates to take care of that sort of thing, boy. We don't need no Mexican to take care of our stable."

Will, now at the open door to the foyer, interrupted. "Major LaMotte, his name is Domingo de la Garza. He is a Tejano and now that your army has won the war, an American citizen same as you and me." Will looked at the two captains and then at Domingo and said, "Show the other officers their rooms while the major and I have a little chat." Will motioned the major into his room and closed the door for privacy.

"What's going on here and why are you in my officers' quarters?" Major LaMotte asked.

"Obviously, you haven't received your latest orders from Washington. Sit down." Will pointed at the chair and small oak desk. "I have a letter from the governor, welcoming you to Texas," Will said, handing him the letter. "Read it and you'll understand."

Major LaMotte read the letter slowly. Then he folded it neatly and said, "Governor Wood thinks I need a Texas Ranger to protect my soldiers. Hell, he knows these men just won the war with Mexico. He was there, leading the Texas Volunteers."

"Major, I know that. I was there, too! The governor didn't send me to protect your soldiers. I'm here to protect the Tejanos. It is our job to keep the peace and not stir up any trouble. There is a lot riding on keeping everyone happy. Once you get your orders, let's have a chat and make a plan to do just that." Will sat down on the cot and swung his lanky legs onto the bare mattress and lay back.

"You know, an officer doesn't lie on an unmade bed," Major LaMotte mumbled as he left the room.

"I'm not an officer!" Will said, then closed his eyes.

Chapter Two

As the sun set over the Rio Grande, a bugler brought attention to the U.S. flag being lowered for the first time at Fort Ringgold. Will watched from the porch as the three officers stood at attention in full military dress. A private blew the bugle, while another folded the flag. Will noticed the native workmen hired to help finish Fort Ringgold seemed in a quandary as to what to do. They just watched. In time they would understand.

Henry Clay Davis, the landlord of Fort Ringgold, had stopped his entourage just short of the fort's entrance. A graduate of West Point, he stood proudly at attention in his carriage for the lowering of the flag. Once the ceremony was over, his driver pulled up in front of the officers' barracks with six armed riders that always accompanied Mr. Davis.

The officers were waiting for Davis. His open carriage had seating for the officers, but they chose to ride their horses, which, after introductions, gave Will and his host time to talk alone. It was a short ride from the fort to the Davis home in the center of the town that was named Rio Grande City. The two-story home was the largest structure in the new town. The Governor had recently appointed Davis to be county clerk, and his home would serve as the Starr County Courthouse until one could be built.

Davis asked, "What do you think of Rio Grande City?"

"It looks like Austin." Will looked around.

Davis said, "Except we don't have a capitol building for the center. We chose the courthouse instead, which as you can see has not been built yet. The sheriff's office and the jail will be upstairs and the county government below."

Will asked, "Mr. Davis, why did you ask the governor to send me here to Starr County?"

"You came highly recommended from a good friend of mine whom you will meet tonight." Mr. Davis motioned the driver to move faster. "Colonel Jack Hays also spoke highly of you. Said that you work well alone, and you will be working alone! I was told about how you procured needed munitions during the Vasquez Campaign. How you went to New Orleans alone to get lead and powder, were stabbed, and damn near died. Yet on your death bed you somehow got the munitions back to Texas. I look forward to hearing that story."

Will nodded his head, thinking, *That is not going to happen.*

They pulled up in front of the Davis home just as the sun sank below the horizon. A crowd of people were waiting. Will had assumed they were going to have a quiet dinner to discuss plans for peace on the border, but the whole town had turned out to greet him and the officers of Fort Ringgold.

A reception line was formed on the way into the house. Davis introduced his wife, Maria Hilaria, to Will and Major LaMotte. He then introduced his business partner, Forbes Britton, who would oversee the setting up of the sutlers store at Fort Ringgold. The last introduction was to a man who looked familiar to Will.

"This is William G. Dryden, editor of the newspaper, who recommended you to us."

Will and "W.G.", as everyone called him, excitedly hugged

and danced a little jig as everyone watched in amazement.

Mr. Davis laughed. "I guess no introduction is necessary."

Seven years had passed since Will Smith and William Dryden had said goodbye on a cold winter night in 1841. Will left Taos the next morning to warn President Mirabeau Lamar in Austin that Mexican Governor Manuel Armijo considered the Santa Fe Expedition an invasion of his territory and that it would be treated as such. Lamar failed to heed the warning and over two hundred men perished. The survivors of the expedition were marched two thousand miles to a Mexico City prison where they would join W.G. Dryden, who had been sent there to serve his sentence.

W.G. and his best friends, John Rowland and William Workman, had been Texas Commissioners for New Mexico. President Mirabeau Lamar appointed them to persuade New Mexico's citizens that annexation by Texas would be in their best interest. Mexican Governor Armijo considered the three men spies for the government of Texas. Dryden spent thirteen months in a Mexican prison to protect his friends from persecution.

The founders of Rio Grande City toasted each other and their guests. A great dinner was served, and a fandango followed with music and dancing. Will and Dryden stepped out onto the large upstairs balcony away from the crowd to talk. A full moon shimmered on the Rio Grande River a short distance away.

"I never thought I would see you again!" Dryden offered Will a Cuban cigar.

"Thank you, Mr. Dryden."

"The cigars are compliments of our host Mr. Davis, and please call me W.G."

Will said, "W.G., I was thanking you for saving my life in

Santa Fe! Once Governor Armijo placed that thousand pesos reward for me—dead or alive—I thought I was a goner for sure."

W.G. shook his head. "The whole damn mess was my doing. Only I could right the wrong that I caused. You just came along looking for the Indians who kidnapped your nephew at the wrong time. You had no idea the political turmoil you had stepped into. I took responsibility for my partners, John Rowland and William Workman. I had recommended them to President Lamar to be Texas Commissioners with me. We had no idea what we were getting into. Then you came along and fell into the mess with us."

Will lit his cigar and said, "You did them a big favor, W.G."

W.G. looked puzzled and said, "What do you mean? They lost everything they had in New Mexico. The trading post and the distillery. They had built an empire."

"You don't know, do you?" Will asked.

"Know what?" W.G. asked, "I don't know whether they're even alive. What do you know? Tell me!"

"They sold out to Ceran St. Varain. They're in California, both families together on the Rancho La Puente in the valley of the San Gabriel Mountains. It's beautiful." Will blew a ring of smoke.

"You've been there?" W.G. asked.

"I found them in the spring of 1843. They purchased forty-nine thousand acres in California near Los Angeles." Will blew another smoke ring.

Overwhelmed, W.G. looked for a chair and sat down. "They're doing good then."

"Yes, W.G., they are, thanks to you. I promised them I would find you, and it's you who found me." Will shook his head and sat down across from W.G. Will pretended not to notice the tears W.G. wiped away with his bandana.

Mrs. Davis poked her head out the door. "I hate to interrupt you, Will, but the soldiers are mounting up to return to camp. Your carriage and driver are waiting." She walked Will and W.G. down to the front porch.

Mr. Davis said, "Goodnight, Will. We have a big day tomorrow; the first company of troops arrives about noon."

Mrs. Davis said, "Thank you, Will, for taking up for my nephew today. Domingo told me what you said to the soldiers today."

Major LaMotte was standing close enough to hear. He had already tied his mount behind the carriage for the return to camp. He said, "Will, I would like to ride back with you. It will give us a chance to finish the conversation we started this afternoon. My new orders were waiting for me; they confirm what you said."

"Good!" Will stepped up into the carriage with Major LaMotte right behind him and they were off toward the fort.

Major LaMotte began, "Will, I'm sorry that we got off to a bad start this afternoon. You and I have a tough assignment. My men and I were trained to be fighters, not peacekeepers. This is my first command since my promotion to Major and I'm totally unprepared for it."

"Major, I can appreciate your situation. Think about mine! I'm the only law there is on the Nueces Strip between Fort Clark and Fort Brown, an area as big as the state of Tennessee. Few Tejanos speak English. How in the hell do you enforce laws no one knows or understands?"

Major LaMotte asked, "Why didn't the government send a U.S. Marshal to the strip? Seeing as the land between the Rio Grande and the Nueces became part of the states after the Treaty of Guadalupe Hidalgo."

Will looked at Major LaMotte. "U.S. Marshals are only sent to protect U.S. territories, like Kansas and Nebraska. Texas was never a territory but a sovereign nation before joining the Union. It's my job as a Texas Ranger to enforce the laws of Texas."

Major LaMotte said, "My job is to protect the Tejanos from the Indians and the Mexicans."

Will muttered, "And neither gives a rat's ass about our laws."

They rode in silence until Major LaMotte spoke. "Will, I overheard Mrs. Davis thanking you for something. What was that about?"

"The stable boy who helped you and your men today, Domingo de la Garza, is Mrs. Davis's nephew. What land the Davises do not own around here belongs to Domingo's parents."

"I see! It was my remarks to Domingo, wasn't it?" Major LaMotte said.

"Yes, that's what it was about. That is why I stopped you this afternoon. Domingo is our best ally in this mission. I would make amends to him if I were you." Will took the last puff of his cigar.

Major LaMotte looked wide-eyed at Will. "You're telling me this young Mexican boy is our best ally?"

Will nodded. "Think about it, Major. He speaks Spanish and we don't. He is kin to about everyone in Starr County. I plan to use Domingo as my interpreter. He's smart and can help us. Someday he will own most of the county."

"What can I do to make amends to Domingo?" Major LaMotte asked.

Will said, "Just treat Domingo with kindness and feed him silver dollars. He has no use for paper money. That's how I know he is smart!"

The major and the ranger agreed they would bury the hatchet and join forces to fulfill their assigned duties. Domingo would be their liaison and interpreter to the city leaders and the residents of Starr County.

Chapter Three

*W*ill slept through reveille. The travel and the soiree the
night before had taken its toll. As he prepared to start
his day, he heard Domingo and Major LaMotte negotiating
for care of the officers' mounts. Major LaMotte agreed to pay
a dollar per officer per week. Will thought, *That is sixteen dollars a month. His Uncle Davis is paying him as much. Domingo is
making as much money as a ranger and doesn't have to furnish a
horse and saddle!*

Someone knocked on Will's door. It was W.G. "Sorry Will,
to bother you so early. I could not sleep, thinking about my
friends in California. I want to join them. This map of the west
coast shows I could sail from Mazatlán to Los Angeles." W.G.
unfolded a map of California. "Would you show me where this
Rancho La Puente is?"

"In the San Gabriel Valley, just below the mountains." Will
pointed.

"Where's their property in the valley?" W.G. asked.

"The valley *is* their land, and most of the mountains on the
west side." Will said.

"All of it?" W.G. raised his eyebrows.

Will nodded and marked where the San Gabriel Mission
was. "Find the mission; their homes are nearby."

W.G. said, "A stage leaves Camargo—the town across the

river—every Monday for Mazatlán about midday. I plan to be on it as soon I can teach someone to take over my job as editor. Why don't you come with me?"

"Thanks for asking, W.G. I would love to see them again, but I'm committed to keeping peace here in Starr County. Thank them for getting my nephew, Fayette, back to Texas."

W.G. asked, "How did they do that?"

"I learned from John and Maria Rowland that they paid the Comancheros sixty silver dollars for Fayette. He was in a bad way. They nursed Fayette back to health then put him on a wagon train back to Independence. He is now with his mother at Washington-on-the-Brazos."

"You went to California just to thank them?" W.G. asked.

Will said, "It's best I let the Rowlands tell you why I went to California."

"I don't understand!" W.G. looked bewildered.

"You will, if John and Maria choose to tell you." Will buttoned up his shirt.

W.G. still looked a little dumbfounded but let it go. "Come and have breakfast with me, Will, at the Rio Hotel. That's where I room and board. Alejandra makes a great breakfast."

Will and W.G. had just finished their meal when they heard the horn of a steamship. Domingo came running in and said to Will, "Major LaMotte asks that you join him and the officers at the landing as the soldiers are arriving from Fort Brown. I have your horse already tied outside."

Will watched from his horse as the first company of eighty-eight U.S. soldiers mustered on the sandy banks of the Rio Grande. The privates were raw recruits who had never seen battle.

Their sergeants, though, were highly trained, seasoned veterans of the Battle of Monterrey. They had been with Major LaMotte when he was severely injured. Each received medals and commendations for saving his life.

A crowd from Camargo and Rio Grande City lined the riverbank to see the troops who had conquered them. It was evident that the señoritas on both sides of the river were attracted to these young soldiers, dressed in their crisp new uniforms and marching in cadence to Fort Ringgold. Will watched the crowd closely for troublemakers, aware that Mexican men who had fought this army during the war might be planning revenge. Many did not return to the Nueces Strip. Some bore visible scars of war, others bore scars no one could see. Those were the ones that Will was concerned about. Most were glad the war was over and the U.S. Army was here to protect them.

A fiesta was planned for the soldiers in Camargo the first Saturday in November, hosted by the mayor. Will and Major LaMotte had concerns about young men fresh off the boat from New Orleans going across the border. Mr. Davis and W.G. feared that not accepting the invitation might ruffle some feathers. It had been Zachary Taylor's soldiers who'd occupied Camargo during the early days of the war. Now Major General Taylor was a national hero and the front runner for President of the United States. The mayor of Camargo claimed to have been Taylor's confidant while the American general had occupied the town.

W.G. lugged a bundle of the *Republic of the Rio Grande* newspaper into the officers' quarters. Major LaMotte and Will were discussing how to explain the laws of the United States to people who couldn't read English.

"I brought enough papers for every soldier to read." W.G. laid the bundle on the floor.

"Let's see what you said about us," Will said, holding out his hand.

LaMotte, a quick reader who knew Latin but not Spanish, quickly realized the paper was bilingual. "This is brilliant, W.G.! How long have you been doing this?"

"About three weeks. This and some legal work is what Clay Davis hired me to do. The papers are free to anyone who wants one."

Will asked, "You mean this bilingual paper of yours tells the story in one column in English, then the next column in Spanish?"

"Yes, that's what a bilingual paper is, Will."

Will jumped out of his chair. "This is the answer to our problem! How often do you print this paper?"

"It's a weekly, Will. Once a week," W.G. answered.

Major LaMotte asked, "Can you print it more often than weekly?"

"If Davis wants to. It's his paper, he can do anything he wants," W.G. said.

From the foyer, Clay Davis said, "I hear you talking about me, W.G."

Davis had come to check on the sutlers store, in which he was heavily invested with Forbes Britton. Davis looked at Will, then Major LaMotte. "What's W.G. saying about me?"

"Would you allow W.G. to publish the paper more than once a week?" Will asked.

Davis said, "Will, you understand that other than the United States Army coming to Rio Grande City, there isn't a hell of a lot of news to report."

LaMotte said, "We have been searching for an answer of how to teach the Tejanos about U.S. laws. Your paper can do that! W.G. is a lawyer and speaks Spanish."

Davis looked at W.G., "Can you do that?"

"Yes, but we need more paper and ink for the press. I'll also need some help."

Major LaMotte added, "We might have a soldier with some printing experience in camp. I'll check on that."

"Let's do it!" Clay Davis said as he headed out the door.

Chapter Four

Will sat at his desk and read the New Orleans newspaper. The month-old article read "Rough and Ready elected President." The story was about Zachary Taylor winning the presidential election. The news would be welcome in camp even though most were confident their hero would win. It was Sunday, the sun high in the sky. Will saw Domingo leading his burro with an old man on it. The man had a large sombrero on his head. His head bobbed up and down with the steps of the burro.

Will went out to greet them. He knew it must be important for Domingo to come on a Sunday, his only day off.

"*Buenas tardes!*" Will patted Domingo on the back.

"Buenas tardes, Señor Will." Domingo gestured toward the old man on the burro. "This is Señor Pedro Lopez Prieto, a neighbor and friend of my family for many years. We seek your help, Señor Will."

Will said, "Well, come on in out of the sun."

The old man slid gently off the burro to the ground. When two officers came out of the barracks, the man trembled in fear and tried to climb back on his burro.

"Señor Prieto, you are safe. No worry." Domingo said, taking him by the hand and leading him up the steps.

Once inside, Will offered water to Domingo and Señor Prieto.

Domingo declined, but the old man smiled and nodded his head.

Señor Prieto told the story as Domingo translated. "His sixteen-year-old granddaughter went to the river to wash clothes and bathe herself. It was last Sunday. I come to visit as I always do on Sunday. Señor Prieto asked me to go find her. I go to where the people wash clothes and bathe. I find the clothes washed and dry, folded neatly in a basket. I look in a clump of willow trees. I found her lying in the grass, her body savagely beaten. She was dead. Her name was Maria Trevino. Her father was Jose Trevino who was killed during the war. Señor Prieto is raising all the children of his daughter, as she died of cholera while her husband was away fighting. Señor Prieto and I ask if you can find the person that did this and put him away forever."

Will saw the anguish in the old man's face. He remembered that look when his own father learned of his son James's murder and his grandson Fayette's abduction.

Will asked, "What side of the river did you find her on?"

Domingo translated and Señor Prieto became agitated and asked, "*¿Por que preguntas?*" which Will knew meant "What does that matter?"

Domingo said, "I told Señor Prieto you would ask that."

The man rambled on in Spanish, which Domingo attempted to translate. "It was on the south side. Why should it matter? A beautiful young girl has been murdered and left to die! She died only a short distance from where she was born on my rancho."

"Domingo, tell Mr. Prieto I agree with him. But he must understand the laws are different on this side of the river."

Domingo translated to Mr. Prieto, who said, "There is no law on my side of the river. Everyone knows that."

Will looked into Domingo's eyes, "Did you know her well?"

He nodded that he did, and tears began to flow.

"Domingo, was she kin?"

Domingo shook his head. "We have been friends since before we could walk. We are only months apart in age. Our parents always say that when we are grown, we should marry. I cared much for Maria."

Will handed Domingo a fresh bandana from the top drawer of his chest. "I will need more information. Tell me everything you know, Domingo!" Will pulled out a tablet and pencil and started to take notes.

"I could see that Maria struggled and fought for her life. Her clothes were ripped off and thrown about the ground." Domingo shuttered, thinking about what he saw.

"Did it look like it was one man or maybe more?" Will asked.

"It was getting dark. I couldn't see the ground." Domingo reached into his pocket. He handed Will a brass button with an eagle on it and a small piece of yellow thread still attached. It was a button from a military uniform. Pulled off in the struggle.

"Where did you find it?" Will reached out his hand. "May I have that for evidence?"

"It was clutched in her hand. They found it when they pre-pared her body for burial," Domingo said, handing it gently to Will.

Will reached for his hat. "Domingo, can you show me where you found Maria?"

On the ferry ride across the river, Will asked, "Did you report Maria's murder to the Mexican officials?"

Domingo said, "We only have the mayor. Camargo has no one like you that enforce the law."

"What did the mayor tell you?" Will asked as they led the horse and burro off the ferry.

"He say it was not his problem and sent us on our way. That is why I bring Señor Prieto to you. I know you will help us."

"Show me the way."

They walked along the creek bank about a mile before Domingo said, "This is the place."

There were no tracks that could be followed. Will looked around the area that Domingo pointed out. Will found a strand of long reddish hair, not the black hair of the Mexicans or Indian tribes.

Will asked, "You know anyone in Camargo with red hair?"

Domingo said, "No, I only see soldiers in the barracks with red hair."

Will rode back to the ferry, leaving Domingo and the old man finishing a makeshift memorial of rocks for Maria Trevino. Once across the river, Will rode hard to the stables. Once his horse was fed and secured, he called on Major LaMotte.

"I need your help, Major," Will said.

"What can I do for you, Will?"

"Call a surprise locker inspection for the entire camp," Will said.

"You sound serious. What are we looking for?"

Will showed Major LaMotte the brass button.

"That's a jacket button off an Army uniform. Nine buttons up the front of every jacket." Major LaMotte looked closely at it. "Where did you get it?"

"It came from the hand of a dead sixteen-year-old girl. She was raped and left on the river like a heap of trash."

Major LaMotte handed the button to Will. "That's terrible! I hope it wasn't a soldier from Ringgold. I will be glad to order the search. It will take time to go through over 100 lockers."

Will replied, "I will make it easy. Muster your troops! I will hand pick the men whose lockers we search."

The bugler blew the call for assembly at the flagpole. The men came scrambling from their tents. An assembly on Sunday afternoon had to be important. Each tent sergeant reported all accounted for except two in sick bay. Will asked the Major to have the men remove their hats, then walked with the senior staff in review of the troops. When he saw a redhead, he stopped and asked them to fall out until all the redheads were in a line. There were eleven men with red hair. The two in sick bay had black hair. A search of their lockers found no fatigue jacket with a missing button.

The remainder were asked to go back to their tents and have their uniforms laid out, buttons up. Every jacket inspected had nine buttons.

"Sorry, Will, that you didn't find what you were looking for." Major LaMotte said.

The next day, Will called on the quartermaster to see if anyone had purchased a button. No one had and his inventory accounted for all the buttons.

The quartermaster was puzzled. "May I ask what this is about?"

Will showed him the button.

The quartermaster said, "You wouldn't find it here at Fort Ringgold. That is a button of the artillery, not the infantry."

"What's the difference?" Will asked.

The quartermaster said, "There is no difference in the button. It's the color of the thread that is hanging and is properly tied as a military issued button, if that helps you."

"Yes, it does, and thank you." Will walked out of the quartermaster's tent knowing the men of Fort Ringgold were innocent of the murder.

Will shared his findings with Major LaMotte, who was pleased his men were not suspects and asked to see the button again.

Major LaMotte said, "I should have examined the button more closely when you showed it to me the first time. I should have seen that this button's thread was artillery. Plus, there is no shine and it's quite worn. This button has been out of service for many years." He handed it back to Will.

Will told Domingo the next day of his findings. The boy was glad that the killer was not from Fort Ringgold as many of the young privates had become his friends.

Chapter Five

W.G. and Will met for breakfast every morning at the Rio Hotel. It was the week before Christmas. The widowed proprietor of the hotel was decorating for the Holy Days. Will noticed the woman, Alejandra, kept looking at W.G. the way Will's mother had always looked at his father. Her attention at the breakfast table was different with W.G. than with the other patrons.

Will said, "You haven't mentioned going to California lately."

W.G. replied, "With having to publish an extra paper in two languages, I can't leave now! There is no one in these parts who can set the press in two languages. I promised Mr. Davis I wouldn't leave until I found someone who could put out a paper twice a week."

Alejandra smiled and poured them more coffee.

W.G. added, "I placed ads in the New Orleans and St. Louis papers. It might take a while to find someone." Will noticed what W.G. said was directed toward Alejandra rather than him.

Will thought, *Something else is keeping W.G. in Rio Grande City.* In any case, Will was excited to have W.G. helping to teach the residents of the Nueces Strip about U.S. and Texas laws.

Will was about to leave when Alejandra's two teenage daughters, Leticia and Sophia, came in the back door visibly upset, speaking rapidly in Spanish.

"Please, W.G., tell me what's happening!"

"Just a minute, Will. I'm getting the story now and I'll translate to you."

W.G. reported, "The girls say they were gathering eggs from the henhouse when two men opened the door and came in on the pretense of purchasing some eggs. The taller man asked to see an egg. When the older girl showed him, he grabbed her around the waist. The younger sister threw eggs at the men. The older sister hit the attacker in the face with the egg in her hand. The girls screamed and the chickens got excited, flying about the henhouse, feathers flying everywhere. The men panicked and ran toward the landing."

Will said, "I bet they are headed for the *Corvette*, leaving today for Fort Brown."

Will and W.G. commandeered a farmer and his wagon, which took them to the landing. The crew of the *Corvette*, a sidewheel steamer, was due to pull out soon for Fort Brown and then on to New Orleans for supplies. It made the loop every three to four weeks, depending on the weather. The captain of the ship was the owner, Richard King, who was just firing up the boilers when Will and W.G. ran up the gangway.

"Captain King, how many men are on this boat?" Will asked.

"Me and a crew of four. Why are you asking?"

"We want to talk to them—now!"

"We're about to shove off!"

"You're not going anywhere until I talk to them. Call them up." Will ordered.

"All hands on deck!" The captain hollered. Two men came

up immediately. Will sniffed them and ordered the captain and the first two crewmembers off the boat. A third came up timidly with eggshells and yellow yoke on his clothes, chicken feathers still in his hair.

"Where's your partner?" Will scowled.

"He's not my partner. I didn't do nothing to those girls."

Will asked, "Where is he?"

They heard a splash from the other side of the boat. Will asked the captain to keep an eye on his crewmen, as Will hurried to the starboard side of the boat. The man came up gasping for air just as Will leaned over the side.

"You got two options: you can come ashore, or swim across the river. If you make it across, there is nowhere to run."

The wet and egg-soaked crewman struggled to shore behind the boat. He wore an old army fatigue jacket. The sleeves were cut off at the shoulder, making it a vest. The bottom button was missing.

A large group had assembled on the landing, including Alejandra and her girls. Leticia said, "That's the man, mamma, that tried to take me in the henhouse." Sophia nodded in agreement.

Soldiers arrived to march the shaggy redhead to Fort Ringgold. Will questioned the other man, who claimed he just happened to be with the suspect when he suddenly went after the girl in the henhouse.

"I thought we were there to buy eggs." The other man described what happened in detail, and his story matched what Leticia and Sophia had said.

The man added, "McDonald has a thing for young Mexican girls. He goes nuts when he sees one and just has to have his way with them."

"Forces them!" Will corrected.

W.G. made notes, as Will questioned the man.

The other man continued, saying, "McDonald liked to brag about what he did with them."

Will asked, "Did you ever see him do anything to these girls other than what happened today?"

"No, but he was always talking about it. He scared me when he told me about breaking their necks." The man shuttered at the thought.

"How many did McDonald say he did that to?" Will patiently waited for an answer.

"He told me so many stories I didn't believe him until—"

"Until what?" Will asked with a growl.

The man hesitated, "What I saw him try with those girls today." The man began to tremble.

Will turned to Captain King and said, "They're staying. You and the others can go, as soon you get me their clothes and gear."

W.G. published the story in the *Rio Grande Republic*. The story made it to San Antonio, New Orleans, and St. Louis. Inquiries came to Will from all over about similar attacks and missing young girls. All along the route of the *Corvette*, which went from St. Louis to New Orleans, Galveston, Indianola, Fort Brown, and Rio Grande City. People wrote and families came to tell of their daughters and wives who were missing. Presumed victims of McDonald, who plied the rivers looking for girls to molest.

Even though the courthouse construction was yet to be started, gallows were erected on the square for all to see.

McDonald was found guilty of murder by the first Starr County jury. The question of where the murder took place was never brought up. Just days before his execution, the prisoner overpowered a guard at Fort Ringgold and broke his neck.

McDonald took the corporal's service revolver and put on his uniform. Then he stole $1,200 from the paymaster's office before making his escape on the commander's best horse.

Now that McDonald had committed several federal crimes, Major LaMotte assigned four of his best scouts to join Will in the search for the fugitive. The five horsemen followed his trail up the Rio Grande where McDonald crossed at Piedras Negras. The U.S. soldiers were under orders not to go into Mexico but had no idea where they were. They gave Will most of their rations and headed back to Fort Ringgold. Will sent Major LaMotte a letter that he was following McDonald's tracks to the Pecos River. He appreciated the military escort but could travel faster alone.

Will had crossed the river here on his way to Santa Fe six years before. He remembered meeting Jean Louis Berlandier, who everyone called "Frenchy." The French-born saloon keeper might be of some help.

Not much had changed at Piedras Negras. Will tied his horse and burro to the hitching post outside the cantina. He entered through the swinging doors, disturbing a sleeping cat on the floor. Four señoritas were sitting with an old man who was crying. They were speaking quietly in Spanish, patting his shoulders, trying to console him. A woman with salt and pepper hair sat behind the bar. She asked, "Can I help you, Señor?"

"You speak English very well." Will put his hands on the bar.

"Yes, and also French and Spanish."

"Is Frenchy here?" Will asked removing his dusty hat.

"Who wants to know?" She asked, eyeing him warily.

"My name is Will Smith. I'm a Texas Ranger looking for an escapee from the brig at Fort Ringgold. I met Frenchy here on my way to Santa Fe in 1842. I thought he might be able to help me."

"I remember you, the Texas Ranger! You were on your way to be married. You showed Frenchy the ring." She laughed. "My name is Norma." She extended a beautiful hand and took his hand and gently caressed it.

Norma tossed her hair back. "Frenchy was my lover for many years. He went back to Matamoros for his wife before the war. I haven't heard from him since." She laughed. "Maybe she kill Frenchy. He told me how much he missed fighting with her. They hated each other, but they loved to fight."

Will nodded. Norma let go of his hand and glanced at the door. "If Frenchy came back, I don't want him. I turned this cantina into a profitable business after he left. The soldiers across the river come with money to spend. I don't need him!"

The old man wailed out a tearful cry.

"I'm sorry, Señor Guerra, I didn't mean to upset you." Norma lowered her voice and spoke to Will. "He lost his daughter, Lupita Guerra, the only family he had. A madman killed her here."

Will asked, "A madman killed her here in the cantina?"

"Yesterday." Norma pointed at the center of the room, "There on my dance floor."

"You saw it?" Will asked.

Norma told Will how the stranger came in happy. Then bought drinks for everyone with American money. She described him as a redheaded, blue-eyed gringo.

Norma said, "He smelled bad. His hair shaggy and dirty. He wore the military pants of a much shorter man."

Will said, "Sounds like the man I'm looking for."

Norma continued, "He drank a bottle of mescal, then gave Lupita money to dance with him. He wanted more from her than a dance. When she refused to leave the cantina with him, he grabbed her by the neck and killed her in front of us. Just like that!" She snapped her fingers, "It happened so fast. Then he was out the door on his horse, heading south."

Lupita's body lay on a table in the back room. Norma didn't know what to do with the corpse. Lupita's father was too distraught to discuss anything after seeing her. The girls, all friends of Lupita, tried to console him.

Word of the murder had been sent to authorities in San Fernando de Rosa, a day's ride southwest.

"I doubt the Mexican officials will send anyone." Norma shook her head.

Will asked, "May I see her body and the money he used to buy drinks?"

"Here is the money. It's so crisp. At first, I thought it might be counterfeit. Do you think it's real?"

It was real. The two five-dollar bills had sequential serial numbers. Ten dollars was a sergeant's pay for a month. McDonald had stolen the camp's payroll. No one would be paid this month.

Norma pulled two dollars from Lupita's bra and called the girls to come to the back room. Will looked at the crisp new dollar bills and said, "That's a lot of money for a dance."

"Yes, it is. The soldiers pay good for the girl's attention. The young men miss their girlfriends back home. They come here to be with a pretty girl. I teach the girls English and how to make men happy."

Will looked a little surprised at what Norma said.

Norma responded, "This is not a whorehouse. I do not allow that here. These are respectable señoritas from good families. They hope to find a man to marry and go to the states someday. They have no future here in Piedras Negras."

33

Norma introduced the girls to Will.

Will said, "I'm sorry about your friend. I promise I will catch this man and bring him to justice."

Mr. Guerra stood at the door, looking at his daughter. "Please find the man that did this," he said in Spanish, but Will understood.

Will said, "I will, Mr. Guerra. First, we must give Lupita a proper burial."

While the girls cleaned her body, Will and her father found a piece of ground under a large willow tree. The nearest priest was days away if one could even be found. Will dug the grave while Mr. Guerra carved a cross with his knife. The girls wrapped Lupita in a blanket that Norma provided. They helped Will lay her body gently in the grave, as the girls prayed. When Will shoveled the last spade of dirt, her father pushed the cross he carved for her into the ground.

Norma closed the cantina and the girls walked Mr. Guerra home. Will and Norma were alone for the first time.

"Will, you have worked hard digging the grave. I have some chili and tortillas I will warm for us."

Will said, "I would like that. Could I clean up before we eat?"

Norma gave him a bar of soap and pointed toward the horse trough outside. She came out with towels and a night shirt, just as he climbed in the water.

"Don't worry! I've seen men naked before." Norma said, smiling, and placed a night shirt and towels on the hitching post. "Don't splash out the rainwater." She pointed at the wooden waterway from the roof top of the cantina, into the horse trough. "If it doesn't rain soon, I will need someone strong to carry water from the river."

Will dried off and slipped the sleepshirt over his head.

When he entered the kitchen, Norma was making fresh tortillas for the chili. He liked the smell of fresh tortillas—and
French perfume. She had prettied herself up. Her hair was
neatly brushed back, cascading below her shoulders. Norma
looked like Will remembered her, when they had locked eyes
for just a moment so long ago. Tonight, there was no Frenchy
to interfere. Capturing a fugitive from justice would have to
wait.

His burro braying and a rooster crowing woke Will from a
deep sleep. He tried to get dressed without waking Norma. It
didn't work. She wasn't finished with him yet. After the morning tryst, she said, "You can go now," and jokingly pushed him
away.

Will smiled and asked, "You're giving me permission to go?"

Norma gave a haughty laugh. "Sometimes a woman needs a
man just like a man needs a woman. Go now and find the man
that killed Lupita."

Will had never known a woman like Norma. Was she serious about just needing a lover at her beck and call? Regardless,
he enjoyed their time together.

Chapter Six

*W*ill had U.S. Army maps of Mexico in his saddlebags. The same maps that guided him through the war now gave Will an advantage over his prey. The tracks of his adversary revealed he wandered about, not sure which way to go, but McDonald always made his way back to the river. Will followed his tracks down the Rio Blanco to the Mission de San Jose del Rio Blanco. The trail led to the front door of the mission. Will searched the grounds and stable. The stolen horse was not there, but signs showed that it recently was.

A priest came out. "You must be the Los Diablo Tejano, Will Smith, the Texas Ranger."

"Is McDonald here?" Will looked beyond the priest toward a trail head.

The priest shook his head.

Will asked, "When did he leave?"

"This morning. Please come into God's house so we may talk." The priest looked out into the woods like someone might be lurking near the creek. Will reached for his carbine.

The priest said, "We don't need guns here."

"The man I'm chasing is a madman. He kills for fun."

Will assumed the priest was looking toward the trail McDonald took. He sensed the fear the priest was trying to hide. He seemed more afraid of Will than of McDonald, something

Will was accustomed to on the Mexican side of the border. Some stories of the Texas Rangers' revenge against Mexican people were true.

The priest said, "McDonald told me of the cruelties the army inflicted on the Mexican people after the Battle of Monterrey. He deserted and was captured by you and was to be executed for desertion."

Will corrected, "We were going to execute him for raping and killing a sixteen-year-old Mexican girl in Camargo. We caught him after he tried to do the same to two young girls in Rio Grande City. He bragged about killing more. When he escaped, McDonald killed the duty guard, a young corporal only twenty years old."

Rather than go inside the chapel, they walked into the small courtyard of the mission. Will rested his carbine on his shoulder, which made the priest uncomfortable.

Will asked, "Did McDonald say where he was going?"

The priest answered, "He didn't tell me anything, except that if you find him, you will have to kill him because he is not going back to jail."

Will said, "I want to take him back alive, Padre."

"To hang him in public! I have heard of this barbaric American custom of taking lives. What does it accomplish?" The priest shrugged his shoulders and shook his head.

Will took a deep breath. "It proves that justice prevails along the border. McDonald was tried by a jury of his peers, convicted in a court of law, and sentenced to death for killing a child! Now he has escaped and murdered at least two more innocent people. Their friends and family need to know that justice will be done."

Realizing this was a waste of time, Will said goodbye and mounted his horse. He had two hours of daylight. The Rio

Blanco forked into the Rio San Antonio a short distance from the mission. Fresh horse droppings confirmed Will was on the right trail. McDonald would probably stop before dark. Will's prey could be around the next bend in the river. He was certain the encounter would come before sunup.

Walking in the dark leading his horse and burro along the rocks of the canyon, Will was thankful for darkness, as McDonald could easily pick him off from the rocks and crevices in daylight.

Will's horse suddenly stopped and shook its head. Will did not teach it to do that, it just did it on its own and had saved Will before. Will watched the ears of the horse twitch about. It heard or smelled something up ahead it did not like. He tied the horse and burro, giving them enough rope to graze. Will retrieved his canteen, carbine, and an extra box of cartridges.

Climbing up on a high point, he saw a campfire in the distance. Will advanced slowly toward it, trying not to stumble on a rock or step on a stick. The roaring fire was suspicious, obviously built to provide light. Long logs were stacked like poles of a teepee. Heat wasn't needed on such a warm night, and a bedroll placed too near the fire for comfort convinced Will it was a trap.

Will patiently waited for McDonald to make the first move. The ranger had stalked renegade Indians, the Mexican Army, and dozens of outlaws. Their moves could be relied on, survival their only goal. But McDonald was insane and driven only by a desire to kill. Predicting his next move was difficult.

By dawn, the fire was only smoldering embers. Will had not slept. His carbine rested on a log aimed toward the campfire. He expected McDonald would soon gather his bedding and ride on. Instead, a curious gray wolf approached the bedroll. It cautiously sniffed and pawed at the bedding as another gray wolf stepped out of the woods. They pulled off the covers to reveal a human body. One wolf started to howl, signaling to its pack food had been found.

Will scrambled down to the campsite where four wolves were about to start breakfast. They didn't appreciate Will's interference with their find. The body was that of a young Indian boy in his teens. His neck had been broken. Will drove the wolves back with some well-placed rocks. The body was stiff but not decomposing. He'd died within the last twenty-four hours.

Will was angry he did not check the bedroll last night. The boy might have been alive. There were no clues as to what tribe the boy belonged to.

Will dug a shallow grave, hitting solid rock after digging only a few feet. He piled rocks on top of the grave to discourage animals from digging up the body.

Now McDonald was ahead of Will between one and eight hours. Setting such a trap indicated the fugitive knew he was being followed.

Will unfolded his map. The Rio San Antonio up ahead made a wide turn of some thirty miles before entering a large canyon, going directly west away from the river. He would come upon the river again in ten miles, but McDonald had no way of knowing that. Going across the bend allowed Will time to set his own trap. The map showed the land desolate and devoid of water, but Will felt confident he could cross it in a day.

Finding a high vista a quarter of a mile before reaching the river again, Will could see for miles in every direction. He watered the horse and burro in a spring-fed creek, then allowed them to forage among the tall grasses near the creek. Tonight, Will would rest. His eyes closed but not his mind, knowing his prey would fight to the death. McDonald had killed a well-trained soldier with his bare hands. Will refused to be McDonald's next victim and was determined to take him alive.

Will found the perfect spot for a trap along the south side of the river. A trail narrowed down to just enough space for a horse to pass. Once in the space it would be difficult to back out. He set a foot snare and covered it with dirt. Once satisfied the snare worked, Will wiped out his tracks with the leafy branch of a willow tree. Now the wait began. Will studied the map, recalculating the distance McDonald had to travel to the trap. It would be in the next day or two. While waiting, he played out every scenario that could possibly go wrong.

Years of waiting for renegade Indians, the Mexican Army, and outlaws had conditioned Will to the art of waiting. He enjoyed the solitude and the anticipation of battle. This wait concerned him more than the others. Once McDonald was subdued, he must be transported two hundred miles to the border.

On the second day, Will heard tumbling rocks, cascading from somewhere up the canyon. If McDonald was that careless, it was a sign he did not expect anyone to be waiting for him. Will used his government spyglass to slowly scan the vast canyon. He spotted a man leading his horse down a trail, far too distant to see his features. They were on opposite sides of the river. Hopefully, the easy low-water crossing would lure the traveler toward Will's trap. Will would only have a quick glimpse of the man before he entered the narrow corridor to the trap.

Will thought, *If the traveler was not McDonald, he was going to be miffed about being caught in the snare!*

The man rode to the entrance of the corridor, where he

dismounted just below where Will stood. The long arms gave McDonald away and the U.S. brand on the horse's left shoulder confirmed it was the stolen horse.

Will held the rope tightly. Once McDonald stepped into the snare, Will jumped down into the corridor to see McDonald, now hanging upside down, rising into the air. Will tied the rope to a willow tree. McDonald now hung like a bat, the snare rope tightly around his legs.

McDonald screamed obscenities as he twisted and turned. "Let me down!" he screamed, his face turning red from the blood flowing to his head.

Will said, "Not until you quit twisting and turning."

Will lowered the snare within two feet of the ground. Will told his prisoner, "Hands behind your back, McDonald."

Once the shackles were fastened securely around McDonald's wrists, Will loosened the snare rope. He then lowered his prisoner's head and shoulders down gently onto the ground.

Will said, "If you try to kick me while I shackle your legs, I will hurt you bad!"

Will had one leg iron on McDonald, who resisted with a hard kick that missed Will's crotch by inches. Will retaliated with a boot to the groin, saying, "I warned you! Get up, McDonald."

"You stomped my—."

"Yep! I did and I thoroughly enjoyed it! Maybe we can do it again."

With the map and compass, there was no need to follow the river. They could head straight east to Camargo, avoiding the town of Monterrey by as many miles as possible. Will had scouted the large Mexican Army camp there three years ago during the war, before the Battle of Monterrey.

Will was busy writing up his apprehension report in his journal.

The date was Sunday, the thirty-first day of December 1849. In a few hours, another decade would arrive. Will thought back on the last ten years of his life. After moving from Coosa, Alabama with his parents, brothers, and sister to Austin in 1839, he remembered living under the family wagon as their cabins were being built. On the twenty-first day of January 1841, Indians killed his oldest brother James, the county judge. His nephew Fayette, the nine-year-old son of the judge, was injured and abducted by the Comanche during the attack. Fayette was taken to Taos, New Mexico to be sold. Will's brother Fenwick would never be the same after witnessing the brutal attack. Indians struck the family again on the seventh day of August 1841, savagely murdering Will's father Thomas W. Smith, the Treasurer of Travis County.

He remembered the night in Taos with the beautiful Bella. Will wondered about their son, named for him, that he would never know. The ghosts of Indians and Mexican soldiers he killed. The whore he shot in New Orleans in self-defense. They all haunted him. Will closed his journal and lay back, hoping to get some sleep.

McDonald asked, "Why don't you ever say something?"

Will said, "Something!" before rolling into his bedroll.

On the move at daybreak, the first day of a new decade, Will unshackled McDonald's feet to straddle the government horse. Will tied it to his, and the burro trailed behind. They traveled single file at a good pace, kicking up a trail of dust.

"Will, what you going to do with all that money?" McDonald asked.

Will ignored him.

McDonald said, "You know you could live well in Mexico on that much money. Just how long would it take a Texas Ranger to make almost twelve hundred dollars? I wouldn't tell anyone you kept it if you was to let me go, I promise."

Will didn't acknowledge hearing what McDonald said. He was busy looking at the big brown cloud rolling toward them at breakneck speed, something Will had never seen, a dust storm.

He found a small outcropping of rocks that had withstood thousands of storms. It would shield them from the winds. Will tied bandanas over the eyes of the horses for protection. The horses were spooked by the viciousness of the storm and their eyes being covered. Will comforted them with a calm, assuring voice. The storm raged on, not relenting until after midnight. He warned McDonald not to fall asleep lying down, something that McDonald ignored.

It was difficult for Will to open his eyes the next morning. For a moment he thought he was blind. His eyelashes were coated with a layer of dust, and moisture from his eyes created a paste that sealed them shut. Gently, Will rubbed them until he saw the mounds of sand were up to the horse's knees and to the burro's belly. Will was amused at what he saw, but his prisoner was not.

McDonald cried, "I'm blind. I can't see!"

"Rub your eyes. McDonald. That crust will break loose, then you'll be able to see this beautiful scenery that came in last night."

McDonald said, "You're laughing, and we were nearly buried alive last night by dirt." He struggled under the weight of the shackles and dirt on top of his body. "Can you help me?"

Will pulled him up to the sitting position. "I told you last night to sleep sitting up."

McDonald brushed off the dust. "I need to piss."

Will removed the leg irons, as it was difficult enough to walk in the sand. Besides, there was nowhere for McDonald to run if he tried to escape. The men chewed on deer jerky as they trudged through the dunes of fresh sand, leading the hungry horses and the short-legged burro. The map showed they were on top of the arid Mesa del Norte. Twenty miles further east they would reach the rim of the plateau. After that they would gradually descend more than a thousand feet into a valley. There the animals could find water and grass. Will knew once into the woods of the valley, his prisoner would have ample opportunities to escape. For now, they trudged slowly on in the sand.

When they reached the rim of the plateau, the sun was setting behind them. In the morning, they would search for the best way down. Will shot a deer that ventured near their camp and they enjoyed fresh cooked venison. There was ample grazing for the horses and the burro. Will turned them loose and in short time they found a spring with good water.

As Will slow-smoked the remainder of venison for jerky, McDonald was kept chained to a piñon tree. He rambled on, asking Will, "Why don't you let me go? If you didn't have me, you could travel a lot faster."

Will quickly pulled out one of the revolvers he wore and fired two rounds toward McDonald.

"Please don't shoot me—please don't!" McDonald cried.

After the smoke cleared, Will approached McDonald and picked up the big rattler he'd shot. He then pitched the dead snake at McDonald.

"Get it away from me!" McDonald screamed.

Will said, "It's dead. Keep it beside you. It will keep other snakes away."

"No, please...get it away from me!"

Will smiled, knowing the vicious killer had a weakness, and it was snakes.

Chapter Seven

*I*n the search for a way off the Mesa del Norte, Will observed a high point on the eastern rim. It protruded out like a narrow finger. The natural formation created by the winds of a million years made a perfect watch tower. Extending vertically for about twenty feet, a large flat rock the size of a small wagon bed sat on top of the formation. A perfect place for observing the surroundings for miles. It was also a perfect place to scout for the best way down to the valley below.

Will climbed the narrow trail created by the feet of nomadic hunters. Scanning the distant horizon, he spotted movement. The spyglass revealed a large cavalry unit of Mexican soldiers. Somewhere between eighty and a hundred mounted men escorted cannons and artillery wagons. Will assumed they were from Fort Monterrey, sixty miles southeast.

Had it not been for the dust storm that delayed their travel, Will and his prisoner would have crossed paths about where the caravan was passing this morning. Will wondered where they were going and what their mission was.

Little did he know, they were searching for him.

Will and McDonald traversed the trail that led down off the Mesa, finding a small stream where they bedded down for the night.

McDonald asked, "Aren't you going to light a fire?"

"No, a fire might attract snakes and we wouldn't want that, would we?" Will rolled out his bedroll. "Take care of your business and be careful where you step. Snakes are all around us."

McDonald stepped carefully away from camp. When his prisoner returned, Will chained his feet to a tree. Neither would sleep well that night. Will fretted about the Mexican Army. McDonald worried about snakes.

At daybreak, Will had the horses saddled. Today they would descend the Sierra Madre to the valley below. Will knew the area, having scouted it for the army during the war.

Will said, "McDonald, you don't want to be talking or making any unnecessary noise—."

McDonald finished, "Because we don't want to disturb the snakes, right?"

Will nodded but did not reveal his amusement at the prisoner's ignorance.

Riding at a steady canter the next day, they stopped only to rest and water the horses and burro. It was dark by the time they reached the river. At daylight they would follow the river north on the Mexican side looking for a safe crossing.

Will was worried. What if the Mexican cavalry he spotted two days earlier was aware he crossed the border searching for a fugitive? The priest at Rio Blanca may have reported him. Norma mentioned word was sent to the authorities at San Fernando de Rosa about the murder of Lupita. The troops could be searching for the murderer of Lupita as well as him.

A Texas Ranger caught in Mexico could unravel the treaty negotiated last year. Will shuddered at the thought of being the person responsible for breaking the Treaty of Guadalupe Hidalgo, which had signaled the end of the Mexican American War.

The Rio Grande was on the rise because of heavy rains along the Devils and Pecos Rivers. Low-water crossings were treacherous. Will knew where the river narrowed and became shallow near the town of Mier.

The citizens of Mier hated Texans and especially Texas Rangers. It was here the rangers were first called "Los Diablo Tejanos."

Eight years ago, three hundred Texians raided Mier two days before Christmas. A bloody battle took place on Christmas day that cost hundreds of Mexican soldiers their lives. But the Texians were outnumbered by the Mexican Army. Thirty Texians died, two hundred surrendered.

The Texian men were remnants of the Alexander Somervell expedition, which was a lackluster intrusion into Mexico ordered by President Sam Houston to appease the Texans who wanted vengeance for the Dawson Massacre. After a punitive raid into Laredo, all were discharged from the Texas Militia and told to go home. Will headed to Santa Fe to find Bella, the love of his life. Three hundred Texas Volunteers chose to continue the punitive invasion into Mexico. The unauthorized looting and pillaging of Ciudad Mier were an embarrassment to Sam Houston and the Republic of Texas.

With a large Mexican Army unit so near, and hundreds of Mier residents that could remember the Christmas Day massacre, Will chose to sneak through the outskirts of Mier in the dark of night. For now, they hid in a clump of willows, with a good view of the road.

McDonald said, "I don't want to travel in the dark."

"What you want doesn't matter. I have the guns and a badge,

while you're chained to a damn willow tree." Will rolled out his bedroll and said, "Rest while you can!"

Lying on his side, Will could watch the activity on the trail between Ciudad Guerrero and Mier. Two-wheeled ox carts came and went carrying farm products to market. Farm wagons loaded with well-dressed families and children passed by. When the church bells began to ring, Will realized it was Saturday the fifth day of January, the eve of Día de Los Reyes, the celebration of the three kings, a holy day in Mexico. Hopefully, everyone would be at mass tonight.

Will quietly saddled the horses and unchained McDonald. They rode slowly toward the river, each animal tied to the one in front. The water below the town of Mier was running swiftly, too high to ford. Now their only option for a safe crossing was the ferry at Camargo.

They arrived at Camargo in the wee hours of Sunday morning. The only things stirring were a couple of mongrel dogs that barked at their horses. Will pitched them each a piece of jerky. It stopped the barking, but the dogs continued to follow them for more jerky. The ferry was moored to two willow trees, one line on each tree. It was a primitive vessel, a simple raft made of timbers tied together by rope, eight feet wide and twenty feet long. Propulsion was provided by the strong hands of a four-man crew pulling the ropes. Will and McDonald waited nearby in the dark for the crew to arrive. The dogs lay near them. Will tossed them the last of the jerky.

Will said, "McDonald, you wanted me to talk to you. So now that our travels will soon be over, let's talk."

"What about?" McDonald gave Will a blank stare.

Will said, "Like how you got your hands around the guard's neck the night you escaped."

McDonald explained, "That soldier bent down to pick

up the keys he dropped outside my cell door. I reached out through the bars; grabbed him and wrung his neck. Then I reached for the keys, opened the door, stole his uniform and gun." McDonald smiled as if he was savoring the moment.

Will asked, "How did you get into the paymaster's office?"

"I didn't know which door went outside. The first one I tried turned out to be the office where the money was kept. There was this big metal trunk on the floor with a lock and chain around it. I tugged on the lock and it was open. There were lots of coins of silver. I took the paper money and left the coins."

Will asked, "Why didn't you take the coins?"

"Coins are too heavy to carry on foot." McDonald tilted his head. "I put the bundles in a money sack and tied it to my belt."

Will asked, "Why did you pick the commander's horse to steal?"

"I didn't know whose horse it was. It was the first one that came to me." McDonald leaned back against a tree.

Will asked, "The commander's horse just came to you?" Will shook his head. "Can you even count to twelve hundred?"

McDonald said, "I can only count to a hundred."

Will said, "Then how did you know it was twelve hundred dollars you stole?"

McDonald said, "I didn't know how much it was until I showed it to this lady in a cantina. She counted it for me and said I had twelve hundred dollars. I asked her what I could buy with it. She said I could buy her cantina for the money I had."

"Who was the woman?" Will asked, even though he already knew the answer.

"Her name was Norma, the owner of the cantina. I spotted this pretty Mexican girl with big dark eyes. I bought her and a bottle of mescal. She was all I wanted. When she pushed me away, I wrung her neck like a chicken."

Suddenly Will could hear horses and men hollering orders in Spanish. The Mexican Army had found them and they were surrounded. A man hollered in Spanish, "*rendirse.*" Will knew the word meant surrender. Will quickly motioned for McDonald to get up and follow him. Will untied the horses and led them to the ferry. The horses stepped onto the ferry with little hesitation, but the burro balked and brayed. The sounds of hooves on the wooden deck of the ferry led the scouting patrol to the ferry. Will pulled out his knife and cut the lines securing the raft. Swift water pulled them into the center of the river. Mexican soldiers could be seen running along the river. The raft ran aground several miles downstream on the U.S. side of the river.

McDonald asked, "Why were the Mexican soldiers chasing us?"

Will realized McDonald had no idea of borders or treaties. The ranger was not interested in teaching McDonald the rules of the border at that moment.

Will said, "McDonald, I reckon they were coming for you, for killing that Mexican girl and Indian boy."

Looking around, McDonald asked, "Where are we?"

"Don't rightly know," Will answered as he helped McDonald onto the government horse for the last few miles of their journey. On a hill overlooking Fort Ringgold, Will heard the call of reveille and watched The Stars and Stripes raised above the fort. A lump developed in his throat; he would soon be home.

Chapter Eight

*O*n Sunday the sixth day of January 1850, Staff Sergeant Dale Jones reported to the commander of the fort that two riders and a burro were headed toward Fort Ringgold from the south. Major LaMotte quickly climbed the four flights of the watch tower. "Let me have the spyglass!" Major LaMotte ordered. The on-duty sentry handed the base commander his telescope spyglass.

"Well, well. It's Will Smith, with the escapee, and by golly—he's got my horse!" Major LaMotte called for the bugler, who met him at the bottom of the tower. "Go to the top of the tower, blow the officers call, followed by the call to colors. Keep blowing the colors loud as you can, until I tell you to stop! Is that understood?"

"Yes sir!" The bugler answered and started his climb.

Soldiers in single file lined the entrance to Fort Ringgold. Worshippers on their way to church heard the bugle call and knew something important was happening at the fort. The first corporal was relieved by a second and a third bugler before Will and his prisoner entered the fort to a cheering crowd.

Major LaMotte yelled, "Welcome home, Will!"

"Thanks, Major. Can you order two of your strongest men to assist me with the prisoner?"

LaMotte ordered his aide-de-camp to pick two men to assist.

When they approached McDonald, he went berserk, kicking the horse in its ribs. The horse bucked wildly and went into a spin. Will had a good hold on the reins of the horse as the shackled prisoner screamed that he was not going back to jail. The horse lunged straight up on its haunches and McDonald went to the ground.

The soldiers pulled the shackled prisoner up and led him toward the guardhouse. McDonald hollered back at Will, "Why didn't you just shoot me?"

Will said, "Sorry, McDonald. The folks in Starr County deserve to see you hang."

Major LaMotte said, "Will, you understand McDonald will have to stand trial for murdering a soldier on my base before you can hang him?"

"I hadn't thought about that." Will scratched his month-old whiskers. "I need to clean up a bit, then go eat a warm meal at the Rio. By the way, I saw the ferry beached on the north side of the river several miles downstream. I'm sure the mayor of Camargo would appreciate your sending a work crew to retrieve it."

Major LaMotte asked, "Will, why don't you join the officers and me for lunch in the mess tent? I'll have Domingo care for your animals and get a crew to return the ferry. The wind must have broken it loose."

Will said, "You best take care of the payroll that's in my haversack first," handing it to Major LaMotte.

"You found the money!" Major LaMotte peeked into the sack, "Is it all here?"

Will turned to answer, "All but a few dollars he spent in a cantina. The corporal's gun is in the bottom of the sack. It was never fired. It seems our prisoner is afraid of gunfire."

In celebration of Día de los Reyes, the cooks at the fort had prepared a feast of beef steak and garden vegetables from the Davis's winter garden. Most of the officers were unaware of Three Kings Day, which is a Catholic holy day in Mexico. Major LaMotte had ordered that all Mexican holidays be observed by the soldiers at Fort Ringgold. He also encouraged the soldiers to mingle and fraternize with the locals, which had so far resulted in three weddings and numerous courtships.

Major LaMotte raised his glass of wine and called, "Here's to Will, the Texas Ranger who brought back our prisoner, my horse, and the paymaster's money!"

The officers cheered, "Hear, hear!"

While they ate, the officers continued to praise Will for his successful adventure. One asked, "Where did you find him?"

Will hesitated, then said, "I found McDonald on the river west of here." Will was never good at lying, but much of his story could never be told. Peace depended on his not revealing his excursion into Mexico.

W.G. interviewed Will about the recapture of McDonald. Will asked W.G. to keep the story short and to the point. "Just say McDonald was recaptured on the river west of Fort Ringgold."

W.G. argued, "Hell, Will! That could be anywhere from here to Santa Fe."

"It's best for all of us, W.G., that you don't write about my capture of McDonald."

W.G. said, "I don't understand, Will. This is the best story since the Treaty of Guadalupe Hidalgo. You are a hero! Everyone wants to read about how you caught this murderer."

He opened his notepad and produced a pencil from his shirt pocket.

Will said, "I have told you all anyone needs to know, W.G. Please, just leave it be!" Will looked out the window toward the river. He saw a detail of soldiers slowly poling the ferry toward Camargo.

W.G. rubbed his chin whiskers as he looked, too, and asked, "I wonder how that happened? That ferry has never broken loose before!"

Will said, "Must have been the wind that done it."

"We haven't seen a puff of wind since you left." W.G. closed his notepad. "I'll write the damn story as you told it. It won't waste any paper, that's for sure."

Chapter Nine

*W*ill and W.G. were having breakfast in the dining room of the Rio Hotel when Clay Davis came in. He greeted them with, "Good to see you, W.G. and Will." The newly elected Texas senator pulled out a chair and sat down. "Domingo told me I could find you both here. I have brought letters from Austin, from your brothers, Fenwick and Harvey. Your sister, Margaret Van Cleve, sent this daguerreotype of her family." He handed them to Will.

"Thank you, Senator." Will said. "When I'm in town, this is where you will find me most mornings. Eating the good breakfast Alejandra prepares for me." Will pushed back from the table as she filled their coffee cups.

Davis said, "You know, Alejandra was married to my wife's brother, who was killed at the Battle of Monterrey."

"You don't say, Senator Davis!" Will knew Alejandra's husband died in the war but pretended he did not. By doing so, he learned Alejandra's husband died in combat, fighting for the Mexican Army. Will thought glumly to himself, *We fought in the same battle; I might have killed him.*

"Will, everyone on the Nueces Strip calls me Clay. Please, just call me Clay. 'Senator Davis' is just too formal for friends."

Will nodded and asked, "What can I do for you, Clay?"

"As you know, in November I was elected state senator of

57

District 21 and R.E. Clements was elected representative. We returned from Austin for the holidays and are heading back tomorrow. Starr County is about organized. The appropriation money to build a courthouse and jail has been approved by both houses of the legislature. Representative Clements and I made our recommendations to the legislature and the governor to fill the county officials' seats for a two-year term. Clements and I want you to be our appointee for Sheriff of Starr County."

"I'm honored. But what about the new governor?"

"Outgoing Governor Wood and incoming Governor Bell have already approved your appointment. Money has been appropriated for you to hire a deputy. Your salary will be six hundred a year and if you accept, Alejandra will give you free room and board at the Rio." Clay looked at his sister-in-law, who nodded her approval.

"Who would I report to?" Will asked, raising an eyebrow.

W.G. answered, "The county judge, the commissioners, and treasurer control your budget. Your boss will be the voters of Starr County, come the next election. Presently everyone thinks you are a hero. I don't know anyone in Starr County that could fill your shoes."

"W.G., you knew about this?" Will's jaw tightened.

"Yes, I did." W.G. shifted in his chair. "It was our intent to make you sheriff from the get-go!"

"Why didn't you tell me?" Will asked, a bit aggravated.

"I was asked not to tell you." W.G. leaned toward Will. "I can keep a secret, you know!"

Clay put his hands on the table. "Will, we had to make sure the people of Starr County would accept you. As an Anglo and a Texas Ranger, the Tejanos had good reason to be concerned about you becoming our sheriff. You have proven to them that you respect them and are here to protect them."

"When would I become the sheriff?"

"You started on the first of January, as far as we're concerned."

Will snickered, "That's two weeks ago! What if I had turned you down?"

Clay leaned back. "W.G., Clements, and I know you like the people of Starr County and they like you." Clay asked Alejandra in Spanish to give Will a room with a good view of Main Street. She nodded and smiled approvingly.

Will moved into the Rio with a view of the lot where Mifflin Kenedy was to build the courthouse and jail. For now, the county business would be taken care of at Clay Davis's home. The Sheriff of Starr County officed at his table in the dining room of the Rio Hotel. Any jury trials would be conducted in the dining room.

The U.S. Army established a weekly mail route between the Forts of Brown, Ringgold, and Duncan. Will and Norma corresponded through the carriers who frequented Norma's Cantina in Piedras Negras.

Norma's weekly letters were explicit and to the point. If Will didn't come soon, she would have to find another to fill her needs. She always wrote the same thing at the end of each letter: "A woman needs a man like a man needs a woman." He wrote her back that he could not leave Rio Grande City until after the military trial of McDonald. He advised things were complicated as McDonald was being tried for the murder of a U.S. soldier. He most likely would be found guilty and shot by a firing squad. The citizens wanted a hanging on the town square. Norma wrote back, "That is crazy. You can't hang a dead man that's been shot. Whichever way you kill him, please cut off his ears. One for me and one for Mr. Guerra, Lupita's father."

Packet ships that brought mail from Washington and points east also brought the newspapers that W.G. depended on to share the world news with the citizens of Starr County. W.G. edited the stories for local consumption but always gave his source of information. Will anxiously waited for the New Orleans *Picayune*, which had the latest news available.

On the front page of the three-week-old paper was the Omnibus Bill of Senator Henry Clay of Kentucky. His Compromise Bill of 1850 was mostly about slavery. Slavery had never existed in the Nueces Strip. The ranchos had *vaqueros* and *campesino* who did the manual labor. They were paid poorly but were free men.

Chapter Ten

*W*ill was meeting with the commissioners and county judge in the dining room of the Rio Hotel. With them was Mifflin Kenedy and Richard King, partners in the shipping company that operated most of the boats on the Rio Grande. They were discussing the possibility of Starr County temporarily leasing the top floor of their warehouse building for the courthouse. It would suffice until a permanent structure could be built on the land Clay Davis had donated. The state legislature had appropriated funds for building a courthouse, but the treasury of Texas had no funds to advance to the county at the present time.

The meeting was interrupted when two uniformed soldiers barged in, asking for the sheriff.

The corporal said, "Sheriff, Commander LaMotte has sent us to escort you to his office at once, sir."

"Can't you see I'm in a meeting with the county board?" Will glared at the soldier.

"Sorry, sir! The commander requested your assistance in this matter posthaste."

Will asked, "What's this about?" as he pulled on his saddle duster.

"I wouldn't know, sir. I was ordered to find you and transport you to his office. We have a wagon waiting for you outside," said the corporal.

Will put on his hat and turned to the county judge. "Whatever you decide is fine with me. I am happy working from here. We do need a jail, though!" Will followed the corporal and his private to the wagon, which another corporal drove. Will knew something big must be up.

At the headquarters of Fort Ringgold, people scurried about from office to office. Once in the commander's office, Major LaMotte excused the messengers and closed the door.

Will asked, "What's going on?"

"Will, I'm sorry, but McDonald is gone." Major LaMotte sat down heavily behind his desk and motioned for Will to sit in front of his desk.

Will uttered, "Son of a bitch! Has the bastard escaped again?"

"No! McDonald died of natural causes early this morning, after being sick for about twenty-four hours."

"Most of the county was coming to his hanging next week! They are sure going to be disappointed," Will said, shaking his head.

"Will, we have a bigger problem! Doc Puryear, the camp medic, said McDonald died of cholera, and we now have nine soldiers in sick bay with similar symptoms." Major LaMotte turned in his chair. "You remember the cholera epidemic we had at Camp Camargo during the war? The Camargo cemetery is filled with more American soldiers than Mexicans."

"What can I do to help?" Will leaned forward in his chair.

"Doc Puryear says we must shut the fort down. No one comes or goes. He says you should quarantine Rio Grande City as well. Put up signs leading into town telling people to stay away. We can't let cholera desecrate this camp like it did during the war. We lost more men to the epidemic than in battle."

"I remember. I was there." Will stood up to leave. "I have to go."

"I know!" Major LaMotte hesitated. "Will, as you will not be coming back anytime soon, I have something for you." Major LaMotte handed Will an envelope.

"What's this?"

"A commendation from President Zachary Taylor for your capturing the murderer of a United States Infantry Corporal. The president also sent you a check for $100.00. It was my intention to present it to you with military honors. With the possibility of an epidemic, it's best we do it here and now." Major LaMotte gave Will a salute.

Will said, "Thank you, Major."

"I'll have my aide return you to the hotel now." Major La-Motte opened the door.

"Thank you, but I would just as soon walk. I have some thinking to do, about how to best handle this cholera matter."

Will got out of Fort Ringgold just as the guards barricaded the entrance. By the time he reached the town square, Will knew what had to be done. He walked into the newspaper office, only to find W.G. and Alejandra in an intimate embrace.

"Excuse me!" Will quickly backed out of the office, as an embarrassed and tearful Alejandra rushed by him.

"Come in, Will." W.G. waved him in. "Now you know our little secret."

"W.G., everyone in Starr County knows Alejandra is sweet on you. It's never been a secret." Will snickered.

"It's important that Alejandra think it's a secret." W.G. sat down at his desk and pointed to a chair for Will.

W.G. continued, "Even though her husband has been dead since the war, Alejandra and her Catholic faith still consider she is a married woman."

Will smiled and said, "I can tell she loves you!"

W.G. said, "I know!"

Will said, "The reason I'm here is I need your help!"

"You mean about the cholera?" W.G. handed Will a proof of a special edition he'd prepared for publication that day.

The headline read "Cholera in Starr County." The front-page story advised readers in Spanish and English what happened at Fort Ringgold. The article on the back page made suggestions to avoid catching cholera.

"That's exactly what needs done! How many papers are you printing?" Will handed the proof back.

W.G. said, "Two hundred for the fort and three hundred for the county. Clay Davis will send four riders carrying them to the ranchos as soon as the ink is dry."

"Thank you, W.G.. I don't know what I would do without you." Will turned to leave.

"Will, I need to tell you something. The reason Alejandra is so distraught is that I am going to California. Since you told me about Workman and Rowland being in California, I wrote Workman. I received a letter back from him last week. They want me to join them. California is growing rapidly. It will soon be the next state. They need legal counsel in some land matters. You know they are the only family I have; we are the 'tres amigos.'" W.G. looked toward the Rio Hotel. "Besides, gold has been found in California! I just might try my luck at gold mining."

"I'll miss you, W.G." Will looked down at the wood floor. "You have been a good friend."

"Likewise, Will." W.G. stood and looked out the only window in his office. "I need you to look out for Alejandra and the girls! I know Clay and Maria will always take care of them financially; she and the girls will never want for material things.

It is their safety I'm concerned about. The Nueces Strip is a bad place for a widow and two young girls. There are some mean S.O.B.s on both sides of the border, like that low-life McDonald who just died! Alejandra told me the girls are still haunted by their encounter with that rat."

"I'll keep a close eye on them." Will put a hand on W.G.'s shoulder. "Why don't you take them with you?"

"I asked Alejandra to marry me. I told her that she and the girls could enjoy the good life California has to offer. She said no." W.G. sat down at his desk. "This is her home, as bad as it is!"

"I am sorry W.G. I know things will work out for you both." Will stood to go. "You remember Captain Jack Hays, the Texas Ranger who led the Texas Volunteers during the war? He is in California. If you see him, please tell Captain Jack that Willy says hello."

"I will do that, if I see him." W.G. started inking his press for the special edition.

Will stopped at the door, hesitated for a moment and turned to ask, "Do you have an envelope?"

"Certainly, this is a big newspaper office, you know!" W.G. joked. "Envelopes in the top of my rolltop desk. Pen and ink there. Help yourself."

Will sat at the desk to pen a letter to his son. A son he would never know. The boy's mother, Bella Miranda, was a beautiful woman of Spanish descent. Her family were the former proprietors of the La Posada Inn on the square of Santa Fe. Her family saved Will from being captured by the Mexican Army. W.G. and friends then planned Will's escape, jeopardizing their own lives in the process.

When Will went back to Santa Fe to marry Bella, he discovered she and her large extended family were in California.

Traveling alone across the Old Spanish Trail from Santa Fe to Rancho La Puente, Will found Bella married to Estevan Martinez and pregnant with Estevan's child. She also had a toddler named William. They had baptized him William Martinez. Three years had passed, and Bella assumed Will was one of the hundreds of Texans that perished on the Santa Fe Expedition.

They'd allowed Will to see the toddler, promising Will that when William was older, they would explain who his natural father was and what had transpired. Will accepted the fact that Bella had married well. His son was in the good hands of a prominent family, founders of Los Angeles County.

Will neatly folded the letter and sealed the envelope with his presidential commendation and the government check inside.

"W.G., do you remember Bella Miranda? Her parents owned the La Posada in Santa Fe." Will handed the envelope to W.G.

"I certainly do. I'm her godfather!" W.G. looked at the envelope, "Can you tell me what's in this?"

"Nope. Your goddaughter can tell you if she wants." Will turned to leave.

"Will, now that McDonald is dead. I've got to know the story of your recapturing him and returning him to Starr County alone."

"I'll tell you sometime. We're too busy today." Will waved as he stepped out the door.

Chapter Eleven

Spring arrived in the Valley of the Rio Grande without a hint of change in the weather. Barrel cactus blooming and the abundance of baby rabbits on the prairie were the only signs of a new season.

Cholera was over for the moment. Early warnings and precautions had saved numerous lives. When the valley people got complacent again, the scourge would return. Will rode slowly through the city cemetery on his way to Piedras Negras. He stopped to look at the fresh mounds of dirt. Under each pile was someone he'd known.

Will was heading to Norma's Cantina after receiving a letter from her that sounded urgent. She needed him and he wanted her.

It was the first time his new deputy was left to keep the peace. Will told those who asked that he was going to Fort Duncan to meet the new commander. It was a half-truth, as the fort was only six miles from the cantina. He intended to call on the commander after a visit with Norma.

Arriving at the cantina, Will saw an ox cart and two oxen tied to the hitching post. Inside he found Norma sitting at a table with two Mexican soldiers in uniform. For an instant, Will was jealous, but Norma's green eyes conveyed to Will she was only thinking of him.

He leaned on the bar and stretched, sore from two days in the saddle. Will needed a drink. Norma excused herself from the soldiers.

"Will, thank you for coming so quickly. I am working alone as I have no help. Would you like some whiskey?" Norma held the bottle for Will to see.

Will nodded. Norma poured him a double shot and whispered, "They will be leaving soon, and I look forward to being alone with you."

"How do you know they are leaving?" Will whispered in her ear.

Norma smiled. "Because they have spent all the money they had."

She went back to the soldiers. After some chitchat, they finished their drinks and left. Norma walked them to the door and said, "Adios, amigos."

Norma came running back across the dance floor. "I'm so glad to see you!"

They hugged and kissed. "I will close the cantina now that you are here." Norma pulled the double doors shut and inserted the board that locked the two doors shut from inside. "Everyone knows when the front door is shut, I am closed." She grabbed Will's hand and pulled him to her living quarters directly behind the bar. Their arms intertwined in the tussle to disrobe each other.

Will said, "No hello?" They both snickered.

"Shut up, Will!" Norma went after him with unbridled passion. Something he had never experienced but did not complain about.

Afterwards they lay back, looking up at the cedar rafters of the ceiling. Norma gasped, "How are you, Will?"

Will said, "Good, now! How about you?"

Norma turned on her side, looking into Will's blue eyes, "I am good, now that you're in my bed."

Will kissed Norma gently. She responded like a mama bear in a beehive. They thrashed about for a while. Then Norma said, "I'm hungry, Will. Would you like some carne asada and tortillas?"

"Yes, I'm hungry." Will heard his horse snicker. "Damn! Norma, you made me forgot about my horse. He's still tied to the hitching post."

Will took care of his horse as Norma warmed their food over coals in the fireplace. They ate leftover beans and carne asada with tortillas. Since leaving Rio Grande City, all Will had eaten was jerky and hard tack. Today's leftovers were a treat for a hungry man.

After eating, Will asked Norma why she needed his help. She explained that the commander of Fort Duncan had issued orders that soldiers not cross the river into Mexico. The restriction was rigidly enforced, which destroyed her business. She explained that American soldiers make more money than Mexican soldiers and they were known to spend their whole paycheck at Norma's Cantina on payday.

Norma added, "The girls who make their money dancing with the American soldiers don't come anymore." She pointed at the dance floor. "That was a place of happiness for the soldiers and the girls. I made money. No more!" She raised her hands in frustration.

Will said, "I will talk to Commander Burbank at Fort Duncan before I leave."

"You know him?" Norma touched his arm. "If he doesn't

allow the soldiers to come across the river, I will have to close the cantina."

Will asked, "What would you do, if you had to close?"

"I have money saved from the times business was good. Maybe I'll just go to California or back to France." She shed a tear.

Will saw a soft side of Norma he had never seen before. He said, "Let's take a walk."

They strolled along the banks of the river, stopping where they had buried Lupita last year. Will saw a fresh grave next to hers. "Whose grave is this?"

"Mr. Guerra, Lupita's father. He died a month after her." Norma made the sign of the cross. "He wanted to be buried next to her." Norma looked at Will. "Did you hang the bastard that did this?"

Will hesitated, then said, "Unfortunately, he died the week before the hanging, from cholera."

"Good! You didn't waste a good rope on him. Did you cut his ears off for me?"

"No, I never got close to his body. The soldiers buried him quickly in the cemetery at Fort Ringgold." They walked in the sand toward the cantina. Will asked, "What would you have done with his ears?"

"I would have given one to Lupita's father. The other I would nail to the wall of the cantina. For all who come, to see what happened to the man that kill Lupita."

"That would certainly get people's attention." Will noticed a mound that appeared to be several years old. He had not noticed it before. When he asked, she seemed annoyed.

"I don't know. It was here when I came."

Will said, "When did you and Frenchy come to Piedras Negras?"

"It was in forty-two. What does it matter?" Norma sounded upset at his questions.

Will spent another night at the cantina. He was admiring the wardrobe of Frenchy Berlandier, the lover Norma shared company with before the war. Will had never seen such fine European clothing for a man. Woolen suits, flannels, and custom-made shirts with collars. Gold cuff links and a gold pocket watch, all stored in a gentlemen's armoire with combs and brushes made of whalebone and deer horn. Will saw a gold Mason's ring amongst the jewelry. Knowing a bit about freemasons, he thought, *No Master Mason would leave his ring and pocket watch.*

Will asked, "Did Frenchy leave all this?"

"He left in a hurry." Norma pointed at the armoire, "Take anything you want. Frenchy isn't coming back!"

"You sure?" Will held up a French made shirt and collar to his chest and looked in the mirror.

Norma said, "It's been four years. Frenchy is probably dead. Maybe killed in the war or by his crazy wife."

"Tell me more about Frenchy."

"I never met his wife, but he was crazy like her. He would take his sketchbook down to the river and draw pictures of plants, birds, turtles, and snakes—all day he would stay! I will show you." Norma handed Will the sketchbooks of Jean Louis Berlandier.

"This is a good picture of you," Will said, after finding a nude drawing of Norma.

Norma said, "Let me see! I never see that picture before!" She looked the picture over for some time. Then she smiled and held it close to her bosom.

Will said, "Frenchy was quite the artist, wasn't he?"

The next morning, Will rode to Fort Duncan to meet Major Sidney Burbank, the commander of the fort. The fort was built on five thousand acres of land leased from San Antonio merchant John Twohig. The meeting was cordial. Major Burbank was aware the popular Sheriff of Starr County was a hero to the Tejano people on the Rio Grande.

Even though San Antonio was the county seat of Bexar County, and Eagle Pass was in the same county, most Tejanos preferred tending to business and legal matters in Rio Grande City rather than San Antonio. The Nueces Strip was their home. They did not cross the border after the Treaty of Guadalupe Hidalgo—the border crossed them. They were now Americans in a Mexican culture and did not understand or appreciate the ways of the Anglos.

Major Burbank said, "Sit down, Will," as he pointed to a chair. "Congratulations on capturing the murderer of Corporal O'Brien. I never heard just where it was you caught him . . ."

"Thank you, Major." Will shifted in his chair, ignoring the question.

Major Burbank waited for an answer that did not come. "Well, what brings the famous Sheriff of Starr County to Fort Duncan?"

"I have a lady friend across the river that has a cantina. She is in financial trouble since you closed the river to your troops."

Major Burbank asked, "What's your interest in my orders to my troops?"

Will knew Major Burbank was a graduate of West Point and a strict disciplinarian. He'd fought in many Indian wars, then the Mexican War. Like many military leaders from the north, Burbank did not understand the plight of the Tejanos of the Nueces Strip. He considered all Mexicans and Indians the enemy.

Will said, "Major, Norma and Frenchy have been my friends for years. They built a business catering to American soldiers' needs."

"I'm aware of Norma's Cantina. Rumor is, Norma killed Frenchy. Obviously, you weren't aware of that." The major offered Will a cigar, which Will declined.

"No, I was not aware Frenchy was dead. She told me he was in Matamoras."

Major Burbank waved his hand and said, "Regardless, I'm not going to look the other way as my men sneak across the river to a whorehouse. I have been told that Major LaMotte and you have an open border policy at Fort Ringgold. The men come and go as they please on a ferry." He struck a match on the bottom of his desk and lit his cigar.

"Yes, and we have no problems with discipline or morale." Will realized Major Burbank was not to be swayed.

Major Burbank said, "Are you insinuating I have a problem with discipline or morale?" He blew a large ring of smoke that floated toward the open window.

"No, sir!" Will shifted in his chair. "I did not mean to insinuate that, Major."

"As you know, in the treaty with Mexico, the United States government agreed we would not send our troops back into Mexico. Whether it was to buy a whore or fight an undeclared war."

Will began, "But sir—."

"Tell Norma, if she wants to cater to my soldiers to open a cantina here in Eagle Pass. We already have two saloons, owned by American citizens. Once she becomes a citizen of the U.S., she can apply for a license, just like they did." Major Burbank flicked his cigar ashes on the floor.

Will said, "Thank you for your time, Major. I will be heading back to Rio Grande City now. Have a fine day."

Major Burbank said, "Give my regards to Major LaMotte when you see him."

"I'll do that." Will nodded and exited the office, knowing he had failed in his attempt to help Norma.

Chapter Twelve

Will told Norma the bad news. Major Burbank would not rescind his order forbidding his troops to cross the river. It was what she expected, and she was prepared for it.

Norma asked, "Can I go with you to Rio Grande City and open a cantina on the American side near the soldiers?"

"Norma, you'll need a building and furniture. I know Clay Davis who owns the town would be glad to sell you a town lot. Maybe even build you a saloon and rent it to you."

Norma said, "I have money to build a simple structure and I have furniture that I can take with me."

"There is just me and my horse, Norma." Will shook his head. "How are you going to get all your stuff to Rio Grande City?"

"Give me two days, and I will have everything in wagons, ready to go!" Norma said.

"Norma, I need to get back to Rio Grande—."

"You don't want me to go with you?" Norma made a pouty face.

"It's just that I have been gone four days already. Another week out of the county…I just don't know." Will looked down.

Norma knew how to get Will to agree, and it worked. After a tryst in bed, she rounded up neighbors to help load everything and found freight wagons for the three-to-four-day journey. She found two wagons for furniture and fixtures and one for the girls and their baggage. Norma recruited six of the prettiest girls from Piedras Negras to come with her, promising them good money and the possibility of finding an American soldier to marry.

Will was concerned about such a long haul over the rocky trail. A teamster for each wagon made four men and seven women. Will knew that on the river road they could be seen by Indians and highwaymen from miles away. They only made thirty miles on the first day due to a broken spoke. They made camp in a clearing near the river, where the teamsters repaired the wheel. The three wagons were pulled together for protection from raiders. Will was not happy with the spot they camped because it was in the open. They had no other option.

After a meal of beans, salt pork, and tortillas, the weary travelers went to bed early. The girls spoke excitedly about the trip; it was their first time away from home. Will and Norma cuddled by the campfire. One teamster stood watch while the others slept. Katydids sang in the trees, and bullfrogs croaked from the banks of the river.

"Tell me about the girl you were going to marry in Santa Fe before the war." Norma cuddled closer.

Will told Norma about his journey to Santa Fe, where he learned Bella had moved to California. He described the mountains and the desert he traveled before finding the San Gabriel Valley where the family had moved. It was difficult to tell Norma about holding his young son. Once he did, he felt better.

Norma said, "It is sad that Bella didn't wait for you."

"She thought I was dead." Will touched Norma's face.

Norma said, "California sounds beautiful." Norma fell asleep looking at a sky full of bright shiny stars.

Will covered her up and relieved the teamster on watch. Nothing out of the ordinary had been seen or heard, which was a good thing.

By noon the next day they had made their way to Indio Creek. Will spotted Indians trailing them from a distance. Most likely a small hunting party of three or four. He did not mention it to anyone, not wanting to create concern. Will was aware they were deep into Indian territory, and several tribes considered the lands around Indio Creek their home. The Indians were not happy about white settlers moving in on their territory. With two loads of furniture, Norma's group appeared to be homesteaders.

They forded Indio Creek and were on high ground when Will spotted about twenty warriors riding hard toward them. He got a better look through his spyglass. They wore war paint and had their short bows, a sure sign that they were not coming for a pow-wow.

Will told the teamsters to pull into an opening in a grove of mesquite. There was just enough room to arrange the three wagons in a defensive position.

"Can you shoot?" Will asked Norma.

"As good as any man," Norma confirmed.

"Good!" Will handed Norma his carbine. "I'm going to see what they want." Will knew exactly what they wanted.

Will rode toward the warriors with his right hand up, a sign he wanted no trouble. Four Indians rode cautiously toward him, all wearing war paint. Two held lances high, making sure the scalps attached were seen. One had a short bow, the preferred weapon of the Apache. The chief held his hand up in the sign of peace. Will saw the red leather sleeves the chief wore from his wrists to his elbows. The huge head, nose, and beady eyes confirmed he was Chief Red Sleeves. Will had seen a poster warning about this tribe's atrocities against white settlers.

The remaining Indians kept their distance. Will glanced back to see Norma and the girls in the bed of the wagon. He hoped the Indians were not aware the heads in the wagon were girls.

But the Indians already knew from their scouts that there were seven women with four men.

Chief Red Sleeves stopped twenty yards from Will, three young warriors by his side. They saw his badge and the revolvers at his waist. They knew Will represented the white man's law. In the land of the Apache, the chief was the law. The chief spoke to a young brave with blond hair and blue eyes.

The blue-eyed brave asked in perfect English, "Why are you here? My father, Chief Red Sleeves, the chief of the Lipan Apache tribe, asks."

"We are on the way to Rio Grande City." Will waited as they talked to each other in Apache.

My father asks, "Why you have so many wives?"

Will knew where this conversation was going and decided to end it quickly. "They aren't my wives; they are prostitutes from Eagle Pass. I have arrested them."

The Indians looked at one another, excitingly chattering at the same time. The chief motioned for them to be quiet.

The son of the chief said, "My father wants to know, how much to buy the prettiest girl?"

Will sat up high in his saddle and said, "Tell your father I will give them all to him if he will take them right now. I am tired of burying them. The men and I would be much obliged if you would take charge of them. Then we can be on our way!"

The son translated to his father. The braves whooped and hollered. The chief raised his hand again for silence and asked, "Why would you do that?"

Will placed his hand over his heart. "Chief Red Sleeves, those girls have the pox in a bad way. There were more of them when we left Eagle Pass, these are the only ones still living. We have buried one or two every day." He looked down, shook his head, and said, "I am afraid I may have caught it, that is why I am staying so far away from you." Will looked toward the long line of warriors behind the chief. "I would not want the wrath of the Apache Nation on me for inflicting the pox on you." Will looked back at the chief and continued, "I have seen the agony this disease inflicted on these girls. I wouldn't wish this disease on anyone, much less the Apache who I know have lost many warriors to the diseases of the white man."

The chief and his son had a rapid conversation. The son said, "The chief asks you to get the teams ready and we will escort you out of the land of Apache."

"I would be much obliged." Will tipped his hat to the chief and rode toward the wagons.

Norma asked, "What's happening?"

Will said, "I think I scared them!"

"How did you do that? They had you outnumbered twenty to one." Norma waited for an answer that did not come.

"Just tell the girls not to smile or laugh. Act like they are sick."

Norma said, "I don't understand."

Will told Norma an abbreviated version of what transpired with the Indians. The Indians followed them until they were far from Indio Creek. They made good time until a U.S. Cavalry patrol found Will and his entourage surrounded by Indians. Major LaMotte, on the urging of Clay Davis, had sent the cavalry in search of Will from Fort Ringgold. When the patrol saw the wagons being followed by a band of Indians, they assumed the wagons and passengers were being taken hostage and began pursuit of the Indians. They ran them back toward the way they came. After a short encounter, the platoon leader rode up to Will.

Will recognized the lieutenant and asked, "What are you doing this far from Fort Ringgold?"

"Searching for you!" The officer looked at the girls who were still acting sick. "What's wrong with them, Sheriff?"

"Norma! Tell them they are well now." Norma told them in Spanish they did not have to pretend they were sick anymore.

The girls smiled and looked flirtatiously toward the officer. The lieutenant said, "Damn, that's amazing!" as he rode off to get his forty-man platoon in formation for the ride home. Norma and the girls were impressed with the military reception. Once the cavalry was in position, the lieutenant asked if the wagons were ready and Will nodded. The lieutenant gave the signal to the bugler who played forward march. The cavalry horses stepped out briskly. Even the oxen responded and stepped up to the bugle's call.

In a short time, Will saw the oxen were quickly tiring out and rode up to the lieutenant. "Call a halt!"

"What's the problem?" The lieutenant asked.

Will said, "Oxen can't move this fast."

"Halt!" The lieutenant raised a hand signal, and the bugler blew the call.

Will pushed down on his saddle horn, relieving the pressure on his backside and said, "Oxen can pull a heavy load all day, but they only have one gait. That is slow and steady. There is a creek up ahead. We need to stop and water the animals and take a little break."

The lieutenant apologized. "I'm sorry, I've never escorted oxen before, just mules and horses."

Will said, "A good horse can travel forty to fifty miles in a day. A mule about thirty. The oxen, maybe twenty, if you want to keep them alive."

"I'm sorry, sir...it's just that—" The lieutenant looked remorseful.

Will asked, "What's wrong?"

"We're out of rations and the men haven't eaten since noon yesterday. That's why we were hurrying."

Norma overheard the conversation and said, "No problem!" She jumped up and started giving orders like a sergeant. She pointed at three privates sitting on a fallen tree trunk. "The three of you, go gather firewood. Pronto!" The girls started kindling for the fire. Soon a big pot of beans started to boil. Will went after meat and brought back a deer and three rabbits. Two girls turned the masa and hog lard into corn tortillas. The soldiers stood in line to get tortillas off the hot grill one at a time. The youngest girl stirred the beans, using a spoon carved from the branch of a nearby mesquite tree. Two girls slowly turned the meat roasting on the open spit. Norma gave each man their choice, whiskey or rum, from the casks of her cantina.

The lieutenant watched to ensure none of the twelve men on night watch took their liquor ration. Army rations for alcohol were a half pint per man, per day. Only after duty and when it was available. Tonight, with kegs from the cantina, supply was no problem. Those who could handle their liquor were allowed extra rations.

Will spoke to the men on watch. He was the most experienced Indian fighter in camp. He described sounds of Indian calls and how they imitated the sounds of owls at night.

Will said, "If you hear the sound of an owl here tonight, wake me!"

A soldier asked, "Why wake you if we hear an owl?"

Will looked at the young private. "Where you from, soldier?"

"Ohio, sir!" The private answered.

Will said, "What kind of owls you have back home?"

"Mostly barn owls, sir."

"I'm not an officer, so don't call me sir! Call me Sheriff or Will." He pointed at the horizon "Do any of you see a barn or a tree other than mesquite shrubs?"

The men on watch shook their heads. Will said, "That's my point. There are no owls because there is no place to hoot." The men laughed. Will said, "What do you do if you hear a hoot?"

"Wake you up!" the soldiers said in unison.

Will explained that his horse would signal if danger approached. Especially if it was an Indian.

"How would your horse know if it was an Indian?" The soldier from Ohio asked.

Will said, "I don't know! Why don't you ask him?"

The men had a good laugh, just as Norma called them to eat. By the time the meal was over it was dark. The Mexican waggoneers brought out their musical instruments. One had a squeeze box, another a fiddle. The youngest waggoneer played a guitar. He was the son of the wagon master, and the nephew of another waggoneer. Their family were all musicians and had played at Norma's Cantina. Norma hoped they might make Rio Grande City their home.

Once the music started, the girls asked the boys to dance, and the party was on.

Chapter Thirteen

*I*t was Good Friday when the Sheriff of Starr County arrived in town with seven attractive girls. The story told was that Will found them and their teamsters alone on the prairie. He was escorting them to Rio Grande City when the Apache near Indio Creek captured them. The cavalry from Fort Ringgold came just in time to save the day. It was the last story that W.G. Dryden would write for the *Republic of the Rio Grande* newspaper. His story of seven girls saved by the sheriff and the cavalry became a sensation in the eastern papers. The notoriety of the event warmed the hearts of the locals, who welcomed the saloon girls with open arms. It was local church leaders who suggested housing the ladies in a surplus army tent on the square until proper accommodations became available.

Will received a letter from his friend George Kendall, editor of the New Orleans *Picayune*. Kendall had read the story in a French paper while on vacation. He wrote that he wished he had heeded Will's warning about the Santa Fe Expedition.

Norma met with Clay Davis at his home. He was excited about Norma moving to his town and the international publicity she unwittingly brought. He learned how Norma had fed the hungry soldiers of Fort Ringgold. He insisted she submit a bill for the food and beverages served. He would ensure that she was adequately repaid for her services and placed on the preferred vendor list for the U.S. Army.

Clay had a vision of something far grander than a simple saloon. He envisioned a two-story hotel, with twice as many rooms as his Rio Hotel. An elegant dining room with French chandeliers for large banquets and room to dance. Norma's Cantina would have gaming tables and a stage for entertainment, built to her specifications. Norma and Clay could become partners, or she could lease the space. For now, he would provide a tent for her cantina on the town square next to her living quarters. Norma was happy.

Clay Davis and his wife Maria Hilaria hosted a farewell fandango for W.G. Dryden, who was leaving for California. Norma and her girls catered the eloquent event at the Davis home. Music was provided by the teamsters that brought Norma's belongings. They'd chosen to stay in Rio Grande City.

Special guests State Representative R.E. Clements and his wife brought Petra Vela de Vidal as a guest. Petra was a childhood friend of the hostess and a cousin by marriage. They had not seen each other since Petra married Louis Vidal in 1840. They and other dignitaries came from Corpus Christi on the *Corvette*. Mifflin Kenedy was then the captain of the steamship. He was a thirty-two-year-old bachelor from Chester County, Pennsylvania. Petra was a twenty-five-year-old widow with six children. This was her first outing since the loss of her husband. She and Captain Kenedy married in 1852. The Kenedys would become one of the largest landholders in Texas.

Like most gatherings where politicians are present, there were speeches. The people of Starr County were anxious to hear how the proposed Compromise of 1850 would affect them. U.S. Senator Henry Clay of Kentucky, who proposed the Federal Act, had never met Clay Davis. The Texas senator's parents were fans of the famous U.S. Senator and named their son after him, but there was no kinship between the two senators. Clay, as the Starr County constituents called their senator, was excited to explain the Texas provision of the five-part compromise.

The federal government might purchase the northwestern border lands.

Most of the guests had no idea where the boundary of Texas would be moved. The Nueces Strip had recently been moved with a line drawn on the map. They were concerned about going through that again. When Clay Davis unveiled a map drawn by W.G. Dryden, the guest of honor, they began to understand Texas would lose the lands east of Santa Fe. The narrow panhandle that went far up into the Rocky Mountains to the forty-second parallel would disappear. Some were against Texas giving up so much territory.

Clay Davis explained, "If the compromise is approved, Texas would then have money to help pay for a much-needed courthouse and jail for Starr County."

Suddenly the party goers were all for the Compromise of 1850. The lands were too far from the Nueces Strip to concern them. The slavery portion of the legislation was of little concern to the people of the Nueces Strip, where slavery never existed under Mexican law. Clay asked everyone to write a note of support for the compromise. He would carry their correspondence to Austin.

As the band played and sang popular Mexican ballads in

the courtyard, the guests sang along with the musicians.

Will found W.G. in the crowd and said, "I would like to talk to you in private."

W.G. nodded and they stepped out away from the house, toward the river. The palmetto trees that lined Main Street appeared to be swaying to the beat of the Mexican music.

Will said, "You asked me to tell you where I caught Mc-Donald."

W.G. nodded, "Yes, I did."

"I went into Mexico…chased the son of a bitch halfway to Mexico City!" Will shook his head, "As mean as he was, he was afraid of snakes and gunfire."

W.G. said, "That's what Clay and I suspected all along. Why are you telling me now?"

"Just consider it a little goodbye gift. One that you can keep in that head of yours." Will pointed at W.G.'s head. "Don't you be writing about that, at least until after I'm dead."

Will reminded W.G. to give the envelope to Bella. He stuttered, "Tell Bella for me, when you get a chance to be alone with her, that I…think of her often."

W.G. gently nodded his head. "Bella looks a lot like Norma. You know that, don't you?"

Will said, "Yes, I noticed that the first time I ever saw Norma at the cantina where I met Frenchy. I was on my way west to find Bella and ask her to be my wife."

W.G. said, "I know," putting his hand on Will's shoulder. "Are you aware the people in Piedras Negras say Norma killed Berlandier in a fit of rage? Then buried him there, somewhere near the cantina?"

Will looked at W.G., "Yes, I heard that. But I don't believe it."

"You don't believe, or you don't want to believe it?" W.G.

raised his bushy eyebrows. "Only reason I told you is I don't want anyone to hurt you."

Will said, "I know, and I appreciate your advice." He wondered who told W.G. but did not ask.

They went back inside to enjoy the festivities.

W.G. left Camargo by stage the next day. He was on a six-hundred-mile journey across Mexico to the Pacific port of Mazatlán, where he would sail to Los Angeles with hundreds of other seekers of fortune. There, as an attorney, he helped perfect the titles to forty-nine thousand acres in Los Angeles County for his friends John Rowland and William Workman. W.G. became the county judge in 1869. He personally planned and built the city's first water works and was the longest-serving city clerk in Los Angeles history.

Chapter Fourteen

*I*t was the seventy-fourth birthday of the United States. The new citizens of the United States on the Nueces Strip went all out to celebrate the Fourth of July in 1850. Fort Ringgold's troops and band marched down Main Street. Flags fluttered in the breeze and excitement was high. The townspeople of Camargo overwhelmed the ferry coming over to celebrate with their U.S. neighbor city. They came by wagon and many on horseback. Most came to celebrate with the Americans. A few came to cause trouble.

Norma's tent cantina on the square was doing a brisk business. Vaqueros from the ranchos demonstrated their riding skills near the river. There was a horse race down Main Street on Saturday afternoon with a purse of twenty dollars, which was a month's pay for a vaquero. It was two month's salary across the river.

During the race, one rider bumped into another, causing both horses to stumble. Neither rider involved won the race, but the incident added to bad blood between the competing ranches. One group was from a Mexican ranch southwest of Camargo. The other from the Davis Ranch on the U.S. side of the border. Drinking added fire to the situation.

Norma asked the Mexican vaqueros to leave her cantina. The leader started turning over tables. He then grabbed one of the cantina girls and said he was taking her with him. Norma came around the bar, her hand in her apron pocket. She told him to let the girl go. He pulled the screaming girl toward the exit. Norma followed close behind, pulling a small derringer from her apron that the vaquero never saw. A clean shot straight to the temple just in front of his right ear. There was little bleeding because the small caliber of the bullet in Norma's derringer did not exit. She touched the artery in his neck to make sure he was dead.

Norma said, "Someone give me a knife!"

A local handed Norma a sharp knife. He thought she was going to remove the bullet. In two short precision cuts she removed an ear. A young vaquero who saw her do it passed out on the floor.

Norma held the ear high, so everyone saw it. "You cause trouble in Norma's Cantina—this is what you get. I cut off your ear, *comprende?*"

The cantina girl ran to Norma and held on to her tightly. Norma looked at the Mexican vaqueros and told them in Spanish to get their friend out of her bar and never come back. Not a whisper was heard as the vaquero's friends carried him out.

Norma yelled, "Drinks are on the house!" The musicians started singing and the girls started dancing. Drinks were poured and everyone continued like nothing had happened.

Will heard the shot from his room at the hotel a hundred yards away. By the time Will got dressed and ran to the cantina, the vaquero's body was on the ferry making its way across the river to Mexico.

Will said, "Norma, what happened?"

Norma said, "A Mexican vaquero started trouble, the son of a bitch. Tried to take one of my girls."

Will asked Norma, "Who saw this happen?" He looked at the crowd. "Who saw what happened here?"

No one said a word. Will looked people straight in the eyes. "What did you see?" They just shook their head or said nothing.

The blood was wiped up and there was no indication that any altercation had ever occurred. Norma went back to tending bar like nothing had happened. Smoke and the smell of gunpowder still lingered in the tent.

Will looked at Norma and sat down at the end of the bar. "Who did you kill?"

"I don't know. We weren't introduced." Norma poured Will his usual and went back to work. Will finished his drink.

Will leaned over the bar. "Could you describe this S.O.B. you say you killed?"

"He is missing an ear and has a hole in his head." Norma said as she wiped the bar.

Will found a trail of blood outside that led to the ferry landing. He could see the ferry was tied up for the night across the river.

Back in the tent, Will realized Norma not only killed him but cut off an ear. *Damn, she is one mean woman. Maybe she did kill Frenchy.* Will went back into the bar and said, "Norma, I want your gun and the ear!"

"You can't have them! I need the gun to protect myself and my business." Norma stood defiantly at the end of her bar. "I'm busy now. We can talk in the morning." She whispered, "After we make love. Go now."

Will turned to see everyone watching. He was uncomfortable with the situation. Norma admitted to killing a man and cutting off his ear. No witnesses, no dead body to confirm it ever happened. *What the hell?*

He went back to the hotel and climbed into bed. It was late

when Norma came and got in bed with him. Will made like he was asleep. That Norma showed no sympathy or remorse bothered Will.

He lay awake thinking of all the Indians he had killed. The prostitute he killed in self-defense on the wharf in New Orleans. He felt no regrets for killing them, for he had no options. Yet he had some sympathy for them.

Will had seen his brother's and his father's bodies after they were savagely mutilated by Indians in separate attacks. Not far from their Austin home, Will found his brother's body and the arrow of the Comanche that pierced through his brother's arm then exited just above the elbow before grazing Fayette's forehead. It happened on Fayette's ninth birthday. His brother Fenwick saw the attack from a distance. Unarmed and on foot, there was little Fenwick could do but go for help. Fenwick had told Will how the attack happened. Fayette had held on to his father's waist as they tried to flee. The horse ran under a tree, knocking them off. Will remembered finding his brothers bloody body and the spot where it happened on the west bank of Shoal Creek. Will thought, *Life was harsh in Austin. Maybe Norma's life in Matamoras was just as difficult.*

He rolled over to see that Norma had gone to sleep crying. Stains on her pillow revealed she did have a heart.

Norma's usual foreplay woke Will from a deep sleep. His first thought of the morning was, *Damn, it would be difficult to arrest this woman.*

It was Sunday morning and, as usual, Will slept late on Sundays. A knock on the door meant it was Alejandra with his morning coffee. Once he heard her steps going down the stairs, he opened the door to retrieve his coffee service. As usual, two cups instead of one. He wondered how Alejandra always knew when Norma was there.

Norma and her girls swam in the cool water of the Rio Grande. It was the third Sunday in July. Will watched them frolic in the river from the wharf. The temperature was over a hundred and not a whisp of wind in the air. Fortunately, the tall willow trees that lined the riverbank gave some shade from the sun. The weather on the Nueces Strip had become unbearable. The river was their only respite from the heat.

Will saw the smoke from the *Corvette's* smokestacks long before the ship was in sight. It was a day early for its weekly arrival. Captain Richard King was at the helm today. He and his partner, Mifflin Kenedy, took turns making the weekly trip up the river to the forts of the U.S. Army.

Today, the U.S. flag was at half-mast. The New Orleans *Picayune* delivered with the weekly supplies told the story of President Zachary Taylor's death on the ninth day of July.

Captain King said, "This is a sad time, Will, for our country. I thought Old Zach was a fine soldier and president." A tear came to his eye as he waved at the sentry in the tower, which meant to send down the quartermaster's wagon.

Will said, "The articles say he died from something he ate at the Fourth of July celebration in Washington."

"All those battles he fought in forty years of service to the Army. Then to die of a bellyache." Captain King shook his head.

Norma came out of the water to greet Captain King. "You're a day early. I have a large order for you. When are you turning around?"

Captain King said, "Not till tomorrow afternoon. You have plenty of time to prepare your order before I leave. I'll be up at the cantina to eat a bit later."

Norma motioned for the girls to head to the cantina. Norma asked, "Will, why is Captain King so sad?"

Will said, "The president died of food poisoning from the Fourth of July celebration in Washington."

Norma said, "He should have eaten at Norma's. Nobody dies of food poisoning!"

Will thought, *No, you just shoot them.*

Chapter Fifteen

*T*he lack of building material and a summer heat wave hindered progress on the new hotel. Workers that did show up accomplished little in the heat of the day.

Few wanted the demanding work of construction life. Unskilled peons were paid seventy-five cents a day. Working on a ranch was easier and paid a dollar a day. Materials shipped from Corpus Christi or New Orleans were unloaded at the landing and hauled up the steep incline to the building site. The hotel project was getting expensive and was far from complete.

Newly-elected Governor of Texas, Peter Bell, called a special session of the state legislature to convene on the twelfth day of August. This emergency session was brought about by the governor's attempts to organize New Mexico Territory's Santa Fe and Worth Counties for Texas. Robert Neighbors, the diplomat who had effectively organized El Paso County, was rebuffed by Santa Fe County officials. U.S. military officers stationed there interceded against Texas. Once Neighbors's report on the situation was published in the press, most Texans wanted to invade Santa Fe and take it.

Clay Davis had been busy overseeing construction of the hotel in Rio Grande City since the legislature adjourned in March. Norma followed the hotel's progress closely, checking the architectural plans, making sure everything was perfect. If it were not to plan, she would bring it to Clay's attention. Clay even allowed her to make changes to some of the plans. When he left for Austin, Davis felt confident Norma could keep the work going in his absence.

Senator Davis met Will at the river landing on the tenth day of August for the first leg of a trip to Austin. They would steam downriver to Brownsville on Captain Richard King's boat. Representative Clements would join them aboard the next packet ship to Galveston. Due to inclement weather, the boat did not arrive until the twelfth. They spent two nights in Brownsville. Fortunately, the hotel had plenty of whiskey and cigars.

Will's presence was requested because Davis wished to meet Will's brother, Harvey, the politically-connected Sheriff of Travis County. The trip to Austin was also the first opportunity Will and his brothers would have to settle the estate of their father, Thomas W. Smith.

Sunset glittered like gold on the Colorado River as the stage from Galveston brought the Starr County delegation to Austin's Bullock Hotel. The legislature had already been in session a week. The hotel had one room left, with two beds. Davis and Clements would share it. Will remained on the stage, which would stay at the stables of his brother, Fenwick Smith, over-night.

Fenwick bounded out of the stable office, which was his home and the Austin way station for the Western U.S. Mail Line. Fenwick was surprised and delighted to see Will stepping off the coach. The brothers had not seen each other in four years.

Fenwick embraced Will warmly and said, "I'm glad you're home, Will!"

Will said, "Good to see you, Fen." Will was the only person that ever called his youngest brother Fen. "It's been a long hot day and I'm hungry. Do you have something to eat?"

"I do! I have cornbread and red beans cooking on the forge. Some whiskey if you like." Fenwick pointed to the outdoor blacksmith forge which served as his kitchen. "I need to take care of the horses and tackle for the line. The coachman and postal agent are already at the beans. You better get on over there."

Will followed the aroma of beans cooking. The driver pointed to the iron bean pot hanging over the smoldering embers. Will spooned out some beans and grabbed a big chunk of cornbread.

After getting his fill of beans, Will took a wooden pail to the community well for water. The cool water washed off the road dust. For a moment, he thought about running down to the river and diving in, just like on summer nights not so long ago. But Will was tired and wanted sleep more.

Fenwick saw his brother staring at the wooden pail. "What's wrong?"

"This is one of those cypress pails father made, isn't it?" Will asked.

Fenwick answered, "That one came from your cabin after

you told me I could have everything in it. Why do you ask?"

Turning the pail, Will remembered the day he and his brothers removed the toppled cypress tree from the Coosa River. His father made toys and pails from it for Christmas presents. That was their last Christmas in Alabama. He dropped the pail when he recalled using it to wash his father's mutilated body.

Fenwick said, "Will, you look tired. You're welcome to my feather bed. I've been sleeping outside under the stars in this heat. Hopefully, you brought us some breeze from Galveston Bay."

The coachman and mail agent were already on the roof of the stagecoach. Will pointed at the red and yellow Concord coach. "They'll be cool up there."

Will and Fenwick chose to sleep on a farm wagon in the middle of the corral. They talked about their brother John and his family that had just moved to Texas. John purchased a plantation on Onion Creek, southwest of Austin. Their brother Harvey came to visit after dark, but finding everyone asleep, he went home to his growing family.

The next morning, Will found Clay Davis reading the Austin *State Gazette* in the dining room of the Bullock Hotel. Will asked, "May I join you?"

"Certainly!" Clay pointed at the only chair not taken in the dining room. Will took a seat across from him.

Will asked, "Where's Mr. Clements?"

"He just left for a committee meeting at the Capitol. The speaker is not happy with us coming late from the valley. I told him we can't control the ships at sea."

Will gave his order to a frazzled waiter, ordering six eggs and a half side of bacon and biscuits.

Will asked, "How are things going?"

Clay answered, "Things are mighty tense! I have been reading the legislative journal. Trying to get up to snuff on the issues. There are legislators ready to go to war with the folks over in Santa Fe. The governor wants us to approve a call for three thousand mounted militia volunteers—to go to war! Hell's fire! The governor of Mississippi says if federal troops try interfering, he will send the Mississippi militia to help us fight." Clay took a sip of coffee. "What do you think about all this?"

Will said, "President Lamar tried invading New Mexico with the Santa Fe Expedition. We know how that turned out, don't we?"

The waiter brought Will's food on a large pewter platter, as it wouldn't all fit on a plate.

Clay said, "You eat." Taking a sip of coffee, he continued, "I'll tell you what I think as you tackle that pig and henhouse full of eggs." Clay snickered.

Will mumbled with his mouth full, "Good eggs."

"I'm glad you like them." Clay shifted in his chair and spoke softly so only Will could hear. "As I was saying, this legislature is looking for war with New Mexico. As you said, we have tangled with them before, we know what that cost us." Clay put his hands on the table. "Will, you were there in the spring of 1841. W.G. told me about Governor Armijo putting a reward out for your head, dead or alive! That was unfair, seeing as you were just trying to find your nephew."

Will said, "They scared the hell out of me. I headed out of Taos in the dead of winter fast as I could go without finding my nephew."

Clay said, "I wish W.G. were here. He was the first Texas Commissioner of New Mexico." He looked at Will. "Wasn't he appointed by President Lamar?"

Will nodded. "What could W.G. do?"

"He had such a way with words. No one I know has a better understanding of the people of Santa Fe than W.G. He could help me persuade these warmongers not to invade New Mexico."

Will said, "W.G. is probably in California by now."

"W.G. is gone forever, I suppose." Clay took a sip of freshly poured coffee. "Will, you were there in Santa Fe. Why do the people not want to be a part of Texas?"

"It's simple, Clay. They are Catholic and speak Spanish! You should understand that, having married into the de la Garza family. Why would Mexicans want a bunch of Protestant Anglos who speak anything but Spanish running their country? It's the same way on the Nueces Strip."

"What you say makes sense. Would you be willing to testify before my senate committee on county boundaries?" Clay asked.

The last thing Will needed to do was get involved in a long political battle in Austin. He had things to do and must make a three-hundred-mile journey home through Indian country alone.

Will said, "You need Jose Antonio Navarro to talk to your committee about invading Santa Fe again. He's your man to talk to the legislators of Texas."

Clay nodded and said, "You're right! I forgot that Navarro was appointed the commissioner and was on the Santa Fe Expedition that left Austin in the summer of 1841."

"It was the seventeenth day of June." Will looked at Clay. "Navarro never had the chance to address the citizens of Santa Fe. He spent three years in prison, longer than anyone on the expedition because the Mexicans considered him a traitor to his own kind. Most likely punished for not deserting Texas, as Juan Seguin had."

Will nodded as he took another bite of scrambled eggs.

Clay said, "Do you know Antonio Navarro?"

Will said, "I never met him. But I know someone in San Antonio who knows him well."

"Who would that be?" Clay raised an eyebrow.

"The man that convinced my family to move from Coosa, Alabama to Texas—Sam Maverick." Will tilted his head and grinned. "That old fart Sam married my childhood sweetheart, Mary Adams."

Clay turned serious, "If the committee approves having Mr. Navarro address us about the situation in Santa Fe, would you go to San Antonio to persuade him to come?"

Will said, "I would. However, I must get back to Starr County soon as we get my father's estate settled." Will reached for his wallet.

Clay said, "I got your breakfast. Go on and take care of your business. I understand your need to get back to Rio Grande City." Clay made a knowing wink, implying Will's hurry was to get back to Norma. Will did not respond to his inuendo.

Will said, "Seeing as no one knows when the session will adjourn, I am buying a horse and saddle from Fenwick. I'll be going through San Antonio. I can call on Navarro for you if you like."

"I'll let you know, Will." Clay nodded.

Will added, "If you want to meet my brother Harvey, he should be at the stables by noon."

"Don't worry, Will. I will find him and introduce myself." Clay said.

Will went to the stables to find Fenwick and Harvey

waiting for him. "Where you been?" the brothers asked in unison.

Will gave Harvey a hug and patted Fenwick on the back.

Fenwick said, "I got coffee, eggs, and bacon for you."

"No thanks, Fen. Clay bought me breakfast at the Bullock. He got me up to date on this matter of our border dispute."

Harvey poured a cup of coffee and asked, "The governor still planning on invading Santa Fe?"

Will said, "Governor Bell is proposing to raise three thousand mounted militia. Get this: he is asking the legislature to approve his taking command of the volunteers! Can you imagine the Governor of the State of Texas, leading the invasion into New Mexico?"

Harvey said, "He's certainly qualified, having been a captain in the rangers, fought at San Jacinto, and a lieutenant colonel in the war with Mexico. That's why I voted for him!"

As Harvey and Will chatted excitedly about the possibility of war, Fenwick listened as he searched through mounds of paper on his desk.

Harvey raised his bushy eyebrows. "This could be the start of something big. We best get prepared for what's to come."

Will said, "You and Fenwick better get to rounding up mustangs as the Army is going to need a lot of horses."

"I found it!" Fenwick handed an official-looking letter to Will. It was postmarked the first day of August at Wilmington, Delaware.

Harvey peaked over Fen's shoulder, "Sure is a fancy envelope."

Seeing the red wax seal embossed with "est. 1802," Will knew it was from du Pont, whom he had not heard from since the end of the war. He opened it gently as to not disturb the seal. Inside was a check for $1,880 and a letter from James

Antoine Bidermann, managing director of E. I. Du Pont De Nemours and Company, better known as DuPont. The check was written on the Farmers Bank of Delaware.

Bidermann sent his regards and advised Will that Alfred Victor du Pont was on a permanent leave of absence from the DuPont company. He, Bidermann, was now in charge of the company. Bidermann inquired as to whether Will wished to remain the agent for DuPont in Texas. "Please advise as soon as possible with an update on the current affairs in Texas." Will had assumed his tenure was over. Bidermann enclosed a price sheet for all DuPont's available munitions and supplies. *How opportune*, Will thought.

Harvey looked at the check. "Will, that's more than three years' pay."

Fenwick looked at the check then looked at Will. "Damn! What did you do to earn that kind of money?"

They noticed a well-dressed man standing outside the stables. He looked like he wanted to come in but was afraid of what he might step in. Fenwick thought he might be from the stage line company and called out, "Can I help you?"

"Do you know where I can find Sheriff Will Smith of Starr County?" the man asked.

Will said, "That would be me."

"Could we speak in private, please?" The man motioned that he wanted Will outside, away from the foul odors of a stable.

"I'll be right out."

The man extended his hand. "My name is James Webb. The governor has sent me to find you. He would like to talk to you."

Will asked, "When?"

"Now would be good. You can join us for lunch." Mr. Webb pointed at an ornate carriage, the driver at the ready.

Will said, "I guess Senator Davis spoke to him."

Mr. Webb said, "I wouldn't know about that. I was just sent to find you and bring you to the Capitol."

They pulled up to the wood plank capitol building that had been built by Will's brother-in-law Lorenzo Van Cleve in the spring of 1839. Will recalled seeing President Lamar swearing in his father and brother James on the wide porch. The legislature met in the chambers on each side of the dogtrot-style structure. The committees met outside under the canopy of the live oaks on the grounds. When the governor saw them, he stepped outside the fortified walls and met them at the gate of the compound.

Governor Bell stepped into the open carriage and introduced himself to Will. "I assume you know Mr. Webb, my secretary of state and a trustworthy confidant. Let's take a ride down to Shoal Creek and pull up under the willows at the crossing."

They stopped at the town's limits where water gently flowed over a large slab of limestone. The slab created a natural bridge, making the all-weather crossing possible. It was at the west end of Pecan Street, only a quarter of a mile from the Capitol and just a few blocks from the stables. Beyond the crossing began the Comanche Trace. It ran northwest along Shoal Creek toward Indian Mountain, the highest point in Travis County.

When the driver chocked the wheels of the carriage and pulled the pin, Will knew it was not going to be a short meeting. Another wagon arrived with four people. Two were armed, the other two brought lunch. The carriage drivers led the horses to deeper water where the animals could drink from the spring fed creek and submerge their bodies in the cool water. Two armed guards kept a close watch on the thicket across the creek.

There was good reason for caution. Seventy-nine settlers in

Texas had died since the last session of the legislature. Twice that number just disappeared, and no one knew what happened to them. Everyone assumed they were done in by Indians.

Will pointed, "You know, the Indians are most likely on the mountains watching our every move."

Governor Bell said, "That's what I've been told."

This was the first time Will had met the governor. Each knew of the other, both having served with Texas Ranger Captain John Coffee Hays.

Governor Bell said, "Will, I have heard much about you, and I like what I've heard. I'm glad you could join us for our daily lunch. This is our favorite place. We try to go somewhere different every day for security reasons, which I'm sure you understand."

Will said, "That's smart, as just across Shoal Creek and up a ways is where Buffalo Hump and four warriors killed my brother James and kidnapped my nephew."

The governor said, "I heard about that, and so close to the capital, too. I'm sorry for your loss."

Will nodded with appreciation.

The governor continued, "At the Capitol, it is impossible to converse about delicate matters with so many ears close at hand. The wallboards are thin. We desperately need a stone capitol like the one in Washington. If Texas keeps growing and new counties are added, we'll need one much larger...with thick walls."

Will listened intently, observing the interactions of everyone present. He was uncomfortable not knowing what this meeting was about or where it was going, but he enjoyed the fried chicken.

The governor finally slapped his knee and looked Will in the eye and stuttered, "Will...I need your help!"

Will asked, "Governor, how can I be of help?"

Governor Bell leaned forward. "I know that during the Mexican invasions of forty-two, it was you that got the ammunition to ward off the Mexicans' attacks on San Antonio! I also know you were seriously injured on the wharf in New Orleans, trying to get the munitions to us."

Will knew that information could have only come from his friend, Captain Hays. Will had warned Hays to never tell anyone about that incident. He hoped the governor was not aware that the injury was inflicted by a prostitute.

Governor Bell looked concerned. "You know, Will, that should be considered a wartime injury and a service-connected one at that." The governor looked at Secretary Webb and said, "James, would you see that Will is honored for his heroism during the Vasquez Campaign? He should also be compensated for his injury."

"Consider it done, sir," answered Secretary Webb.

Will stuttered, "I appreciate your consideration, governor, but...I wish you wouldn't do that!"

Governor Bell asked, "Why would you?"

Will said, "I have my reasons, Governor! Let's talk about your needs. It's getting warm and I have other business to tend."

Governor Bell was surprised Will turned down his offer. "Very well then! As you probably know, I am attempting to raise an army of three thousand men. Many able-bodied young men have written me that they are ready to come forward to protect our borders." The governor looked at his secretary and said, "James, please tell Will what we need."

Secretary Webb said, "Will, we have the manpower!" Webb looked down at his shoes. "We somehow must acquire arms and ammunition." He looked forlornly at the governor and stuttered, "For the...large army...that Governor Bell will personally command. We understand you're still the acting agent for DuPont in Texas. Is that correct?"

Will nodded, wondering where they got that information, as he was just informed this morning that he was still DuPont's agent for Texas. That was too much of a coincidence.

"We need blankets, tents, and supplies for a winter invasion into New Mexico."

Will said, "Du Pont can furnish that as well as uniforms. At least he has in the past."

Governor Bell said, "Will, this conversation must be kept in the strictest confidence."

Will affirmed, "What you tell me, stays with me."

Governor Bell looked again at his secretary. "Tell Will everything he needs to know!"

Secretary Webb said, "Will, we don't have the financial resources to purchase provisions for a large army."

Governor Bell added, "James means the State of Texas is dead broke!"

Will said, "Governor, everyone in Texas knows that! Starr County was appropriated money to build a courthouse during Governor Wood's administration. We have yet to receive a penny."

Governor Bell said, "It's much worse, Will." The governor looked at Secretary Webb, who seemed nervous about discussing Texas's financial condition. "The only purveyor we have recently paid is DuPont for the ammunition you got us in the spring of forty-two. Mr. Bidermann wrote that he was going to file a claim against Texas for the money owed if we didn't pay immediately. We knew a lawsuit and claim from DuPont would reach the press. Then the whole world would know how broke we really are!"

Will thought, *Now this is making some sense. That's why I just received payment and Bidermann made sure I was still the agent. Damn, he is smart!*

Governor Bell asked, "Will, we are asking you, as the agent of DuPont and once the personal bodyguard of Alfred du Pont, can we get credit for our war needs?"

Will said, "Get me an itemized list of your needs. I will let you know as soon as I speak to Bidermann."

Secretary Webb said, "Here it is, Will. The list we made before the special session."

Will said, "Governor, I ask that our correspondence and negotiations are strictly confidential. I will be leaving for Wilmington, Delaware soon as I can procure a horse and saddle for the ride to Galveston."

Governor Bell said, "I can have a carriage take you."

"Thank you, Governor, but I can travel faster on horseback. I know the way."

"Thank you, Will!" The governor said. They shook hands and Secretary Webb returned Will to the stables in a separate carriage.

Chapter Sixteen

oseph Lee, a family friend and attorney, waited at the stables for Will to return. Lee needed Will to sign papers to settle the estate of his father. Will signed the documents and penned a letter to Norma. Then he wrote a letter asking for a temporary leave of absence as the Sheriff of Starr County.

Will then went looking for Fenwick. He found his brother in the corner of the corral, bent over, shoeing a horse.

Will said, "Fen, I need the fastest horse you got that's ready to travel."

Fenwick put the horse's hoof down and removed its tether. The horse standing between them was in the way. Fenwick slapped its rump to move, and it did with a kick. Fenwick stretched his aching back, placing the farrier tools in his leather apron.

Fenwick said, "The fastest horse here would be *my* horse, Will! I wouldn't sell her, but you're welcome to take her and bring her back."

Will said, "I don't know if I will ever be back." He looked around the corral and added, "Tell me what's for sale."

Fenwick said, "This sounds serious, Will! What's the matter?"

Will said, "All I can tell you is I have to make a long trip.

Don't ask me any questions, Fen. I will write as soon as I can. One thing I can tell you is it's important I have a good horse."

Fenwick shook his head and bit his lip, trying hard not to ask another question. He pointed toward a good-looking stallion. "That blue roan's got a good head, stout legs, stands two hands higher than anything I've got. No one that I know has ever rode him."

Will reached for the rope in Fenwick's hand. "Fen, get me a saddle, nothing fancy, just comfortable with a good blanket."

Will spoke softly to the horse. It snickered as he slid the rope over its head. Will continued to stroke the horse, and it liked Will's touch and calm voice.

Will saw Fenwick coming out with an armload of tackle. "What else can you tell me about this horse?"

Fenwick said, "Not much! Harvey found him with a herd of mustangs on the river near Hornsby Bend. He was with them long enough to become the leader of the herd. Once Harvey got a rope around his neck, he led him back to Austin and the other horses followed him into the corral. Just like a Judas goat."

Will said, "I can tell this horse is not wild. Rambunctious, maybe, and a little horny. We should do well together." The horse did not resist as Will laid the blanket on its back. It snickered with excitement when Will cinched the saddle tight. "I think he wants to be rode."

The horse stood perfectly still as Will mounted him gingerly.

Fenwick opened the corral gate wide. Will rode out onto the dusty street. Walking the horse slowly at first, then a slow gait, then a fast gait. The horse wanted to run, and Will let him trot up Pecan Street to the Bullock Hotel. Will turned him and raced back toward the stables.

Will asked, "How much for this horse?"

Fen opened the gate. "I can't sell him, Will! Especially now since you showed me how well-trained the horse is. I'm sure he belongs to someone! He might have wandered off looking for a mare in heat. Harvey and I have posted signs all over town, but no one's claimed him."

Will dismounted, dropping the bridle on the ground. The horse had three white stocking feet and white spots on its hindquarters. A well-muscled stallion over sixteen hands tall. The horse watched Will intently as he walked around it, admiring its composition. The untied horse stood erect and never flinched when Will walked behind.

"I need this horse!" Will looked pleadingly at Fenwick.

Fenwick rubbed his goatee. "It's not branded, been here over a month, and no one's claimed it . . ." Fenwick looked at the horse then at Will. "Just take him and the tack."

Will smiled and said, "Thank you, dear brother. What do I owe you for the tack?"

Fen looked at Will, "Just a damn good explanation of why and where you're going is all I want."

Will saw his younger brother was upset. "In good time, Fen." The horse followed them and the brothers had a good laugh when they turned around. It shook its head excitedly.

Fen said, "I will gather you some grub for the trail! You better write."

Will nodded, "I'll write you, if you introduce Harvey to Clay Davis for me. The senator wants to meet him."

Will stopped at the Bullock Hotel. Senator Davis was out, and no one knew when he would return. He left the sealed letter for Norma and his request for a leave of absence with the desk clerk with instructions to give them to the senator when he came in.

111

Will and the horse he'd named Blue stopped by the City Cemetery a mile east of the Bullock Hotel. The wooden crosses still stood. Will thought, *My father and brother have a good view of Austin from here.* It would be the last time Will would visit their graves.

Gay Hill in Washington County would be Will's next stop. The community was named for two families that first settled there, the Gay and Hill families. But the long, hot day ended before he reached his destination. He could have continued, but Will was concerned about the huge crevices in the earth, results of the drought. A horse or person could break a leg or worse stepping in one of the cracks in the dark. He chose a high ridge to sleep in hopes of getting a whiff of the gulf breeze.

The howl of a coyote woke Will before daylight. Deer jerky and a hard biscuit with a sip of water was breakfast. Will led Blue ten miles on the dusty trail until the sun was above the horizon. Will stopped at Yegua Creek, where he watered Blue and let the horse graze along the creek bank. He hoped to reach Gay Hill by noon. He wasn't sure his brother James's widow still lived there. Gay Hill was where the last letter from his sister-in-law was postmarked. Will was hopeful he would find Angelina Smith and her children, Fayette, Caroline, and Lorena. It had been eight years since Will had seen them.

Blue was a curious horse. He pawed at his silhouette in the water of Yegua Creek. Will laughed at the horse trying to figure out the image in the crystal-clear water, not yet understanding that he was looking at his own reflection. Blue pawed the water gently, making ripples. Will recognized the moment when Blue understood it was his reflection. The stallion snorted, shook his long mane, then pranced along the creek bank admiring what he saw.

Suddenly Blue stopped in his tracks. The horse saw movement in the mesquite thicket above the creek. Will turned toward the swishing sound he heard. He recognized it was not the sound of a four-legged critter. Will knelt in the thick brush while Blue kept his gaze on the same spot, his ears erect, slightly rotating in search of sound. Will waited and listened, but heard not a sound. If it was Comanches, they would be making the calls of a crow.

Will's carbine was in the scabbard tied to the saddle on Blue. Both revolvers were around Will's waist. The horse instinctively moved slowly toward Will, never taking his eyes off the point of curiosity. Will had no idea what Blue would do if shots were fired. He did not need a run-away-horse. Will instinctively made a slight ticking sound with his tongue. Blue moved closer. When the horse stopped, Will continued making the clicking sound until he could retrieve his carbine and get the bridle on Blue. A horse whinnied above the creek bank. Whoever they were had the advantage of higher ground.

Will heard the familiar cock of a gun from a distance. He hunkered down lower, waiting for a shot that did not come. It meant the shooter was locked and loaded, waiting for Will to make a move. Will picked up a good-sized rock and hurled it about ten yards away into thick brush. Boom! The high caliber sound and thick blue smoke revealed the shooter was using a muzzleloader. Will listened to the gun being reloaded and counted the seconds it took the shooter to reload. He counted to two hundred before he heard the click. Just about three minutes to reload. Will kept calm and considered his options. Is the shooter alone? Do they have a repeating handgun?

Today, Will could not make a mistake. Many depended on him to get arms and ammunition for Texas. Will decided to take a chance. He called out, "What do you want from me?"

The shooter shouted back, "Everything you got worth having!"

"I don't want to die!" Will pleaded. "Come and get it and just let me be. You can have everything I have, just don't hurt me."

Will snickered at seeing the shooter lumbering down the creek bank., alone with only a rifle. A powder bag on a lanyard hung around his neck. He made out a boy barely old enough to shave, carrying a loaded and cocked rifle down a steep incline. Will thought, *No one is that dumb.* The musket was a foot longer than he was tall.

Will heard the gun fire. Then watched the boy tumble down the incline. Will walked over as the boy shook off the dirt and picked up his hat.

Will asked, "You alright?"

The boy snarled, "You promised to give me everything you got. Now let me have it. The horse, your money, your guns."

Will looked at the boy and laughed.

"What's so funny?" The boy asked.

Will said, "That was when you had the drop on me. Your gun is now up there," pointing up the hill, "unloaded. And you are down here." Will made a quick draw of the guns he wore. "I have two Colt revolvers and a carbine."

Will took pity on the boy, who appeared to be in a state of starvation. There were sores and blisters on his face and hands.

The boy, in apparent desperation, lunged at Will, who was a foot taller and outweighed him by sixty pounds. Will stepped aside and tripped him as he went by. The boy turned and came back toward Will. This time Will grabbed him by his long shaggy hair. "Are you crazy?" Will asked, holding him by the hair.

"You're making fun of me, and I don't like it." The boy tried to kick Will.

"You're not in any position to not like what I say or do, young man. What's your name?"

"None of your business!" The boy kicked at Will his last time.

Will picked up the screaming boy and threw him in the creek.

The boy shouted, "I can't swim, I'm drownin'!"

"Tell me your name."

The boy said, "My name is John, and I can't swim!"

Will said, "Stand up, John. The water in Yegua Creek isn't over your head!"

The boy looked surprised when he quit trying to swim and stood up.

"I'm glad to make your acquaintance, John." Will looked at the boy, "My name is William Witherspoon Smith; my friends call me Will. You can call me Sheriff Smith. When you come out of the water, I am going to arrest you for armed robbery. I could also charge you with trying to steal my horse. Either one of the charges is a hanging offense."

John looked about to cry. "Are you really the sheriff?"

"Yes, I'm a sheriff and was a Texas Ranger before that." Will flashed his badge. Will wanted John out of the water. "You best get out now, before that water moccasin over there gets you."

John came stumbling out of the creek mumbling, "Just my luck...first damn time I ever try to rob someone, I pick the sheriff."

Will said, "Trust me John, I have arrested many a criminal in my day. I can honestly say you don't have what it takes to be a robber."

John asked, "Do you think they'll they feed me in jail?"

"Certainly. You get fed two meals a day. Up to the day they hang you."

"Then let's hurry, cuz I'm hungry."

"When was the last time you ate, John?"

"I don't remember. I ate some pecans I found a few days ago."

Will handed John his haversack that had the last of his jerky and a stale biscuit. "This will have to do until we get to Gay Hill."

John greedily bit off a piece of dried jerky and tried to chew it fast and almost choked.

Will asked, "Is your horse up there?" pointing up the embankment. John nodded, as Will mounted Blue and told John, "Don't forget your musket on the way up."

John looked surprised at Will. "Ain't you afraid I might get it and shoot you?"

"You won't be shooting anyone with that gun!" Will motioned for him to start moving..

John stopped and turned around, "Why are you so sure I won't shoot you?"

"Your powder's all wet!" Will laughed. John didn't appreciate his humor.

At the top of the slope, Will tied the emaciated old horse to Blue's saddle horn.

Will asked, "John, where are your folks?"

John said, "They all dead."

Will said, "I am sorry for your loss. When did that happen?"

John answered, downcast, "A few weeks ago. They died of cholera."

Will looked at the boy wide-eyed and asked, "You lost

everyone in your family at one time?"

John said, "No...they died one at a time for about two weeks straight until...well, I was the only one left."

John had just turned sixteen. His parents were John and Mary Day. They'd come from Missouri with Stephen F. Austin. John Day, Sr. had fought at San Jacinto and patented his bounty for a section of land in Washington County. Cholera had swept through there and wiped out many of the early settlers and their families. John Day, Jr. lost not only his parents but two brothers and a sister.

Will asked, "What about the bounty of land your father had?"

John said, "I traded it to our neighbor, Mr. Barnhill, for this horse." John spurred the sad-looking horse, which did not respond.

When they got to the hilltop that overlooked the valley where John's home had been, nothing remained but smoldering ruins of what had been a dogtrot farmhouse with a chimney on each end. The stone chimneys were all that were left of the Day home.

John whispered, "It's gone." He started to cry. "They burned down our house. Everything is gone."

Will asked, "Where does this neighbor Barnhill live?"

John said, "The next farmhouse across the creek. Why do you care?"

Will looked serious. "I want to talk to him."

They rode along the creek as John pointed out the boundary between the Day and Barnhill property. John said, "That's Mr. Barnhill's house over there."

Will said, "I want to meet this Mr. Barnhill."

Barnhill saw them coming and came out of his cabin, holding a rifle. He shouted, "What can I do for you, mister?

And don't bring that boy near my family. He is a carrier of cholera."

Will said, "My name is Will Smith and I'm a friend of Mr. Day, Jr." Will got off Blue and started to thank Mr. Barnhill for what he did to help the Day family. Will extended his hand toward Mr. Barnhill for a handshake. As Barnhill extended his hand, Will grabbed the gun barrel and threw him to the ground in one swift motion.

Will saw the wife and children watching. Will said to Barnhill, "Smile at them and wave like we're just clowning around, I don't want to embarrass you in front of your family." Will motioned for John to follow them to the smokehouse.

They entered the smokehouse where turkeys, hams, and sausages were hung to cure. Will pulled a ring of smoked sausage off a hook and handed it to John. "Here is something to eat, John." Will smiled at Mr. Barnhill. "When someone is sick or dies, a good neighbor is supposed to take food to the survivors. Not burn their house down."

"I had to, on count of the cholera! I didn't want my family catching it. Everyone died 'cept John, and he don't look well. I'm afraid to be around him. That's why I told him to go away and not come back."

Will said, "He is starving and thanks to you, homeless." Will turned to John and said, "Go check on the horses."

When they were alone, Will said, "Barnhill, I didn't see any graves on the place. Where did you bury the bodies?"

Barnhill said, "I left them in the house when I set it on fire. That's what I thought was the safest thing to do. I didn't want my family catching it. John traded his property for the horse he is riding."

"You're such a good neighbor, Mr. Barnhill," Will said sarcastically and got in his face. "Trading that broken-down horse for a fine home and six hundred forty acres of prime farmland that his father fought for at the Battle of San Jacinto."

Mr. Barnhill said, "He seemed happy when I made the deal with him. The boy put his mark on the bill of sale. I will show you if you want."

"He's only sixteen years old. He can't read and he was distraught. You took advantage of the poor boy, and I am not going to let you get by with it."

Barnhill asked, "How do you plan to do that? I got the law on my side, ya know!"

"How is that?" Will asked.

Barnhill said, "I know my rights, and who the hell are you to interfere?"

Will explained to Barnhill that he was a lawman and had just come from a meeting with Governor Bell in Austin. That he could arrest him for larceny, burning a poor orphan's home, and desecrating four human bodies. Barnhill's face drained of color.

"What do you want me to do?" Barnhill sat down on a stump.

Will asked, "Do you have a church here?"

"Yes, I am a deacon at Mount Prospect Presbyterian Church in Gay Hill."

Will asked, "Are you a Mason?"

"Yes, why do you ask?" Barnhill looked at Will suspiciously.

Will said, "You asked what I want you to do. This is what I ask you to do! Go to church this Sunday and pray for forgiveness for what you have done to John Day and his family. Then I want you to call on the other deacons and your Masonic brothers to help you rebuild this young orphan's home. I want you to teach John to read and write, to farm and be self-sufficient. I expect his new home to be ready by Christmas."

Will continued, "If it's not finished, I'll be calling on my good friend Reverend Hugh Wilson to discuss whether you should be outed or not from the Presbytery."

Barnhill stuttered, "Where...do you know the reverend from?"

"We came to Texas together. Hugh and I stopped in San Augustine for a few weeks. He stayed there for a while with my brother Mitchell Smith to build the first Presbyterian Church in Texas. I plan to call on the reverend in Gay Hill. I will tell him the great plans you have for rebuilding the Day home. I know he will be delighted to know of your good deeds."

Barnill nodded and looked contrite.

Will asked, "Now, would you mind if I took a smoked ham and two smoked sausage rings? John and I are hungry."

Mr. Barnhill nodded again, and they parted cordially.

Chapter Seventeen

*J*t took most of the afternoon to make it to Gay Hill. John's horse could not move very fast, and Will feared the animal might go down at any moment. If it did, they would never be able to get it up again. John was in no condition to walk.

At the Gay Hill Store and Post Office, Will received directions to Angelina Smith's home. It was the next house down from the Post Office on the road to Independence.

The sun going down gave little relief from the heat and humidity. The doors and windows were wide open at the home of Angelina Smith. Her guinea fowls screeched, announcing their arrival. Angelina came to the door. She stared...could it be?

"Is that you, Will?" Angelina called out.

Angelina came running out in her bare feet. Will immediately recognized her. They hugged as Caroline and Lorena watched timidly from the doorway.

Angelina said, "Come, girls, this is your Uncle William who we always called Will." Angelina saw the sickly-looking boy on the poor old horse. "Will, who is this boy?"

Will said, "Angelina, that's John Day, Jr. I found him today on the banks of Yegua Creek. He is in a bad way. Lost his family to cholera a few weeks back. His neighbors burned the home.

I'm trying to find him shelter until Christmas."

Angelina turned to John and asked, "You're Mary and John's son, aren't you? They're members of Mount Prospect Presbyterian, where we go. Your family is gone, John?"

John nodded. Angelina said, "I'm so sorry." She grimaced, "Will, let's get John off this horse, he needs something to eat and lots of rest." Angelina and Caroline lead John into the house. Lorena showed Will to a horse pen behind the house.

Will handed Lorena the ham. "You don't remember me, do you?"

Lorena said, "No, but I sure know who you are. I'm glad you're here." Will hugged his niece who looked so much like her mother.

"Where is your brother, Fayette?"

Lorena said, "He works at the General Store in Washington-on-the-Brazos and lives upstairs over the store. Mr. Shackelford made Fayette the manager last spring. We're proud of him. He comes home on Saturdays after the store closes and spends Sundays with us."

Will said, "Thanks for showing me where everything is. Lorena, can you take that ham inside to your mother? Tell her its cured and ready to eat. I will be in as soon as I take care of the horses."

Lorena said, "You have a good-looking horse, Uncle Will."

"Thank you, Lorena."

Will entered the house to find Angelina and the girls at the table entertaining John while he ate. His color was much improved, and his demeanor had changed for the better. John had washed up and had on a set of Fayette's clothes. It was the first time Will had seen the boy smile.

Angelina fixed Will a plate and they ate together. They talked about their trip from Coosa thirteen years earlier, when the three generations of Smiths came to Texas together. John and the girls went outside to watch lightning bugs in the dark.

Angelina said, "Caroline is starting as a freshman at Baylor next year." She picked up the plates and placed them on the sideboard. "I am not happy about her going to a Baptist school, but Reverend Wilson says it's the best Christian school west of the Mississippi. Lorena will be finishing her studies at Independence Female Academy next year, where I teach. The pay's not much, but my girls got a good education for free. Schooling here is much better than that old oak tree in Austin."

"How is Fayette?" Will changed the subject before Angelina started to cry about the horrible death of her husband and Fayette's abduction by the Comanche.

"Fayette learned his trade as a merchant and is managing Shackleford's Store at Washington-on-the-Brazos." Angelina beamed with pride.

Will said, "He turned out good for all the boy has been through. I plan to see Fayette in Washington on the way to Galveston tomorrow."

"Galveston!" Angelina said, "John thinks you are taking him to jail. That's what he told us just before you came in. Tell me you're not going to do that!"

"No! That is just what I told John. My way of teaching right from wrong." Will divulged what transpired on Yegua Creek, about John's attempt to rob him, the swindle of his father's headright of six hundred and forty acres, and the burning down of his house.

Angelina said, "Will, please leave him with me. I'll teach him to read and write. I'll make sure Mr. Barnhill does what you told him to do. If he doesn't, I'll call him out in front of the whole congregation."

"Thank you, Angelina, I had hoped you would feel that way about keeping John. I am headed on a long journey and don't know when I will return."

"Where are you going?"

"I can't tell you, Angelina." Will bit his lip. "I promise to write when I can and tell you about it."

Angelina looked hurt. "It must be important then. Please be careful and know we will be praying for you."

John and the girls came in, followed by the girls' dog Becka, named for their Grandmother Rebeckah Smith.

Angelina said, "Will says he won't take you off to jail if you stay here with us."

Caroline and Lorena looked at John, "See? We didn't have to ask!"

"I guess that's a yes." Will said, looking at a smiling young man and two happy girls.

Will woke to the sounds and smells of a woman in the kitchen. Angelina cooked Will a breakfast of eggs and bacon with fresh biscuits and gravy. She cut up some of the ham, boiled a few eggs and would add some biscuits for good measure on the road.

Will said, "Just enough to get to Galveston."

Angelina asked, "How long will it take you to get to Galveston?"

Will replied, "It's usually a two-day journey by horse or stage, if it doesn't rain."

Angelina scoffed, "Not much of a chance of that!"

Blue was in the horse pen when Will came out. Both were eager to get on the trail. He fed the horse a small ration of oats, saving the remainder in case they found no forage on the trail.

John came out to say goodbye and to thank Will for all he had done for him.

John swallowed and said, "I'm sorry that I tried to steal your horse and rob you. I was desperate. I don't know how to thank you for bringing me here."

Will said, "John, you're in a good home with good people. You help Angelina and the girls with the men's work and protect them from harm. They will need wood chopped for cooking and warmth come winter. Offer to help where you can. It will make you feel good, helping them." Will knew John was still weak on his legs. "Let's sit down." Will pointed toward a large tree stump.

John asked, "Do you think Mr. Barnhill will keep his promise to build my house back?"

Will said, "Angelina and Reverend Wilson will see to that! You understand you let Mr. Barnhill take advantage of you, don't you? Let that be the last time you let anyone hoodwink you! Your father risked his life for that land fighting Santa Anna at San Jacinto. That section of land Texas gave your father on Yegua Creek is worth at least six hundred dollars. Farming cotton, you could make that every year, once it starts raining again. Soon you will have a home. Not many young men your age have a home and a plantation. I notice you have an eye for the girls. Find you a good woman, John, get married and have a passel of children."

"I just didn't think I was worth much." John rubbed his heel in the dry dirt.

Will put a hand on John's shoulder. "You are worthy, John! Remember to do things that would make your parents proud even though they're no longer here. It will make you a better man."

Angelina overheard the conversation but acted like she didn't. "John, your breakfast is on the table."

John asked, "Can I hug you, Will?"

Will opened his arms and Angelina opened hers and they all hugged for a while before she said, "John, the girls are waiting to eat with you."

John smiled and headed to the house that would be his home for now.

Chapter Eighteen

Will discovered Washington-on-the-Brazos had become a prosperous town. That had not been the case when the family arrived there the year after Texas Independence.

The Smith family had assumed Washington-on-the-Brazos would become the capitol of Texas. Before they could unpack, they learned President Lamar was considering Bastrop for that honor. The Smiths were hell-bent on being wherever the center of government was to be. They moved first to Bastrop, then moved up the Colorado River to Austin, one of the first families to settle there.

Will tied Blue to the hitching post of the Shackelford and Gould Mercantile Store. It was more than a general store, it was a trading post, like the Taos Trading Post where Fayette apprenticed at the age of nine. Will saw several people inside. A young clerk said, "I'll be with you soon as I finish this order." Will recognized Fayette. He looked just like his father James had at eighteen.

Fayette finished up with the customer and turned his attention to Will. Once Fayette got a good look at Will, he knew who he was and shouted, "Uncle Will, it's you!"

They hugged and patted one another.

Will looked his nephew over and said, "You've grown up to be quite a man. I recognized you the moment I saw you."

He stopped short of telling Fayette he looked like his father.

Fayette asked, "What brings you to Washington-on-the-Brazos?"

Will said, "To see you! Who I haven't seen in...um, nine years." Neither wanted to remember. It had been on Fayette's ninth birthday they'd last seen each other.

Fayette turned his head to the rear of the store and yelled, "Watch the store while my uncle and I go outside!"

Someone in the storeroom said, "Will do, Fayette!"

Fayette shuffled his way slowly to the front porch of the store.

Will said, "I am proud of you, Fayette. I read about your trip in the eastern papers. I came home the same route. Your adventures on the Santa Fe Trail with Peter Duncan had to have been exciting for you." Will could tell Fayette didn't want to talk about his captivity and quickly changed the subject. "Now you're home, taking care of your mother and sisters." Will teared up, "I'm sorry, Fayette, that I couldn't find you when I was in Santa Fe."

They sat down on the wooden bench. From the porch, they had a view of the main road through town. A farmer's wagon passed by and everyone waved.

"Uncle Will, don't beat yourself up about not finding me. You couldn't have found me, because you were headed back to Texas before I was brought in by the Comancheros. I was told how the Mexican Army thought you were a spy. The reward for you was dead or alive."

Fayette greeted a customer going into the store, then continued, "The Rowland and Workman families were already considered spies for Texas. John's brother, Thomas, was in prison for treason. They were under orders to not communicate with Texas in any way."

Will nodded and said, "You and I were caught up in a war we knew nothing about! I carried the resignations of the commissioners back to Austin." He shook his head. "I warned President Lamar that Governor Armijo considered the Santa Fe Expedition an armed invasion of his territory. Only Fenwick and Harvey heeded my plea!"

Fayette said, "Uncle Fenwick told me how you saved them from the terrible fate of the Santa Fe Expedition."

Will said, "My good friend George Kendall went anyway, over my objections. He survived the expedition to be captured by the Mexicans, then marched fourteen hundred miles from Santa Fe to Mexico City to serve thirteen months in prison."

They both sat, thinking how fortunate they were to have survived that winter of 1841.

Will broke the silence. "I found an orphan boy on Yegua Creek two days ago. He was in a pretty bad way. About like you was when the Rowlands took you in. I want you to help make something out of John Day."

"How?" Fayette looked at Will.

"Maybe he can help you in the store. He doesn't know much about anything. Your mother is going to school him. He could use a big brother. Now that you are here all week, John can help your mother and the girls with the chores. John owns a section of land on Yegua Creek that one day will be a grand plantation. I hope you can help him."

Fayette said, "Uncle Will, the Rowlands took me in and cared for me. They taught me a thing or two. Maybe I can teach John Day to be a merchant."

Will said, "That would be good."

Fayette asked, "Where are you heading on that fine stallion?"

"He is the best horse I've ever rode." Will told Fayette the story of how his Uncle Harvey found Blue on the prairie east of Austin. Running with a herd of mustangs.

Fayette said, "Wait…I received a reward poster about a blue roan with white stocking feet. As I recall, it's a large reward." Fayette searched the community bulletin board the store maintained on its covered porch. He found the weathered poster and handed it to Will.

Will read it and said, "No doubt about it, Fayette. This description is this horse! They offered a hundred-dollar reward for it." Will shook his head. "I would give a lot more than a hundred dollars for that horse."

Fayette asked, "Where did you say you were going?"

Will said, "I didn't say, but I'm going to Galveston next." Will read the poster again. "The poster says the owner is Jacob Haller of Chappell Hill."

Fayette said, "I know him. He's the postmaster and they own the new Stagecoach Inn at Chappell Hill. It's the next stage stop, south of here about eleven miles."

Will grinned and said, "I'm glad you showed me that reward poster. If I rode Blue through Chappell Hill, I might have been lynched for stealing the postmaster's horse!"

They heard the stagecoach rolling into Washington. As soon as it stopped, the coachman stood on his board and yelled, "There is Jacob Haller's horse!" Will and Fayette looked at each other.

"We know, Luke!" Fayette said to the coachman, Luke Snyder. "This is my Uncle Will who brought the horse down from Austin."

"I know Will! He is the Sheriff of Starr County! We took him, Senator Davis, and another fellow to Austin just last week." The boisterous coachman helped his only passenger, a well-dressed young woman, down from the coach. Will decided riding the stage with her might be interesting.

Will said, "Good to see you again, Luke. I will be going with you to Galveston, after leaving Mr. Haller's horse with him in Chappell Hill."

Luke said, "I'll be glad to take him for you!"

"I'm sure you would, Luke. But it was my brother, Sheriff Harvey Smith, that found the horse. He would want me to return it personally to its rightful owner."

They both watched as the pretty woman made her way to the privy. Luke whispered, "I'm sure glad she didn't want us to get her trunk down." Luke pointed at the only luggage on the stage.

Will and Fayette gazed up at the largest trunk they had ever seen. It could easily hold two grown men.

Luke said, with a wink, "You bein' the law, you get to ride free!" Then he spoke loudly, "I didn't know Harvey Smith, the Travis County Sheriff, is your brother!"

Will said, "Thanks to you, Luke, now everyone in Washington County knows that." Luke did not understand Will's sarcasm and thought it was a compliment.

Luke said, "Well thank you, Will!"

"You're welcome, Luke!"

The young woman heard the exchange as she approached the coach. She tried to hide her amusement with her hand fan. Luke helped her up into the coach. She and Will made eye contact; both suppressed their snickers. Luke didn't have a clue.

Fayette said, "Uncle Will, I must get back to tending the store. Thank you for stopping by to see me. Write me when you can." They hugged and Fayette shuffled back into the store.

Will unsaddled the horse, then helped the mail agent put the saddle and tack on the top luggage rack next to the huge steamer trunk. The saddle and tack would be delivered to Fenwick's stable on the next trip. Blue was tethered to the back of the coach. Will didn't know if Blue would trail the coach or fight being behind it. Inside the coach, on the back wall, was an oval window the size of a dishpan, that opened inward. Will could watch Blue from the front bench, but the lady passenger sat in the center of the back bench, blocking the view and what little breeze the opening would allow.

Will asked, "Would you mind moving just a bit where I could open the window for some air?"

The lady was fanning her face with a pearl-handled fan. "More air would be nice. I can move over if you allow me to set my bird cage next to you." She handed over a cage that contained a white pigeon and a white rabbit. "I must keep them up high for the breeze. I don't want to lose my precious babies to the heat."

The lady moved just enough that Will could open the window. Just as he secured it against the wall, Luke lurched the stagecoach forward, throwing Will into the woman's lap. Will ended up on the floor in his attempt to get off her. The bird and the rabbit were on the floor but still in the cage. Will managed to get upright on the bench directly in front of her. She was as amused as Will was embarrassed. They both began to laugh uncontrollably.

Blue stepped in perfect cadence with the team and followed along amicably. Will found it difficult to keep a watch on Blue with such a pretty face sitting across from him.

She said, "Why are you staring at me so intently?"

Will said, "Actually, I'm looking at the horse! Should he step in a hole or stumble, he could be dragged to death by the stagecoach." Will held the stopping club tightly in his hand and explained, "This club is for pounding on the roof in the event that were to happen."

The lady passenger asked, "Sheriff, you're quite fond of that horse, aren't you?"

"Yes, I am, Mrs.—"

"It's Miss! Anna Belle Fontaine. My friends call me Annie."

Will said, "May I call you Annie?"

"Yes, please call me Annie. You worry considerably for a horse that isn't yours. She turned to look at Blue, as a gust of wind blew in some unwanted dust particles.

Annie said, "Oh, my...something is in my eye!" She tried to wipe it with a hanky she pulled from her sleeve. After several tries in the bouncing coach, she couldn't remove the dust.

Will banged on the ceiling with the stopping club. Luke started braking the coach with the foot pedal and hollering "Whoa, dammit!" at the team of horses. By the time Luke got the team stopped and the door open, he found Annie with her head in Will's lap. Luke misconstrued the situation totally. His eyes went wide and he slammed the door. Will was only trying to remove a particle of dust from her eye. Luke again gave them a good laugh. Annie said, "You Texans are hilarious!"

Will asked, "Are you sure I got that bugger out of your eye?"

"Bugger in my eye?" Annie snickered.

Now that they were stopped, Will took the opportunity to check on Blue. The horse was now covered in a thick coat of dust and lather, its eyes and nostrils muddy. Will thought, *This is no way to treat a fine horse on such a hot afternoon.*

Will said, "Luke, hand me down the saddle. I'm riding Blue in from here. Where is the nearest watering hole?"

Luke said, "The Brazos River crossing is only a half mile ahead. The passengers usually get in the water to cool off."

Will saddled Blue for the last time, cleaned the animal's eyes with a bandana and climbed onto a happy horse. "I will see you at the Brazos," he said, waving to Annie.

Will and Blue were wading in the river long before the stagecoach arrived at the crossing. Most of the caked-on dust was washed away in the water. Will did not let Blue drink his fill of water; just enough to get the dust in his mouth down. Will cleaned the horse's caked nostrils and around the eyes. Blue seemed to recognize he was near home.

The Brazos River looked inviting in the one-hundred-degree heat. Annie was already in the water. Her bird cage hung in the shade of a pecan tree. Will decided a swim in the Brazos with Annie might be fun. Leaving his guns and outer garments hanging on the coach door, Will waded into the water as Luke and the mail agent stood guard.

Annie looked at the two men. "Why don't they come in the water and get cool with us? They must be burning up."

"They can't leave their post," Will explained. "They are on guard to protect us from the Indians."

Annie asked, "Why don't the Indians want us in the water?" She looked at Will for an answer.

Will laughed, thinking she was joking, but she was serious.

Annie asked, "Why would the Indians care if we swim in the river?"

Will said, solemnly, "They don't want us here, in or out of the water. They want to kill and scalp as many white people as they can. It's just the way it is! Until we can kill every last one or drive them away, we must constantly be on guard."

Annie looked genuinely puzzled. "Why can't you just live in peace with one another?"

Will said, "Annie, my nephew Fayette, the cripple boy you saw at the general store, was captured by the Comanche on his ninth birthday. His father was scalped in front of him. They cut Fayette's Achilles tendons to keep him from running.

They disabled him for life! My brother and father were killed and scalped by the Indians! It's just the way it is here."

"Will, you're scaring me!" Annie climbed out of the creek and changed clothes behind the stagecoach.

"I didn't mean to scare you. But you're in Indian territory and you need to be alert."

Will dressed and mounted, spurring Blue to head south. "I will see you at the inn." It would be Will's last ride on Blue and he intended to make it a good one.

Chapter Nineteen

he Stagecoach Inn at Chappell Hill had just been
completed and had all the latest accoutrements of fine
living within its fourteen rooms. Will's arrival set off a commotion inside. Someone bounded down the stairs. Will heard
an agitated woman's voice say, "Someone will be out shortly."

The town's founders, Jacob and Elizabeth Haller, owned
the two-story inn. Jacob was the postmaster at Chappell Hill
and Elizabeth and her mother, Charlotte Hargrove, ran the
inn that catered to the travelers on the Smith and Jones Stage
Line.

Blue was happy to be home. He let everyone know he was
there, expecting to be seen, petted, and adored. A young black
boy of about fifteen came out. The horse recognized the boy
instantly and demanded his attention by pawing the ground,
shaking his head, and snorting. Will knew his Blue was home
where he belonged. He uncinched the saddle as the boy greeted the horse.

The boy said, "Mister Haller is sure gonna to be glad to get
Titan home again."

Will asked, "Where is Mr. Haller, and who are you?"

"My name be Tobias. Mr. Haller is behind the barn, milking. I can take you if you like."

Will said, "Yes, please take me to him."

Tobias led Will and the horse to the back side of the barn. Jacob Haller was under a Jersey cow, milking her. From under the cow, Jacob recognized the stocking feet of his horse. The excited innkeeper jumped up and tripped over the pail of milk that he and the cow had worked so hard to produce. The man muttered a curse but set his attention on Will when he saw him.

Will said, "I believe this is your horse, Mr. Haller."

Jacob Haller said, "Yes, that's my horse, Titan! Where in the world did you find him?" Jacob rubbed Titan's nose and the horse licked the fresh milk off Jacob's hand. "I have searched everywhere for him."

Will said, "I didn't find him. My brother, Harvey Smith, the Sheriff of Travis County, found him with a herd of mustangs. Just east of Austin at the bend in the river they call Hornsby Bend."

"What's your name?" Jacob wiped his hands on the milking apron he wore before shaking hands.

"William Smith is my name; my friends call me Will." From the handshake, Will knew Jacob was a Mason.

Jacob asked, "May I call you Will?"

"Certainly, please do."

Will sensed Jacob's tension and recognized his anguish after hearing a cry from the house, "Jacob, we need that milk now!"

"Tobias, will you finish milking the Jersey? Now don't kick the bucket like I did. We need all you can get for dinner tonight and breakfast in the morning. The inn is full and we're expecting a crowd for Miss Fontaine tonight."

Will asked, "Annie Fontaine?"

Jacob nodded and said, "We know her as Anna Belle Fontaine. Do you know her?"

"Yes, we rode in on the same stagecoach from Washington

-on-the-Brazos. Your horse and I took a swim in the river with her. She was quite an entertaining traveling companion."

Jacob said, "Good to hear, as I have dinner guests who have paid a good price to be entertained."

Will said, "Your horse and I rode ahead of the stage to see if the horse knew the way home. He brought me straight to you. Annie and the stage should be here any moment."

Jacob said, "Then I must get this milk to the kitchen. Please stay for dinner and an evening of Miss Fontaine! I will get your reward money. I must get things ready for our guests, and that includes you."

"Thank you, Jacob. I don't expect any reward and my brother, being the sheriff, doesn't either. My younger brother Fenwick boarded your horse for a couple of months. I'm sure he would appreciate a few dollars for feed."

Jacob said, "Fenwick the saddle maker is your brother? Those saddles on the rack, he made."

They could now hear the stagecoach in the distance. Jacob said, "I must help my wife get ready for our guests; she is with child and needs all the help she can get. I'm sure you know what that's like." Jacob grabbed the half bucket of milk from Tobias and headed for the inn.

Jacob stopped and turned around. "Tobias, you take care of things for the incoming stage. Your father can't help you. He is busy cooking bread in the kitchen. You know what needs done!"

Tobias had started to brush Titan's matted coat of horse-hair. Will held out his hand and said, "Let me, Tobias. I'm the one that rode him. I should do the brushing. Besides, you got chores to do."

Will patiently brushed Titan. Both enjoyed the tender strokes of the curry comb. The stage pulled up under the porte-cochere of the inn. It took Luke and the mail agent and a servant to get the steamer trunk down from the stagecoach and into the inn. Will wondered what in the world was in that trunk.

Tobias said, "You best grab you a bucket of water from the trough while you can. Once those thirsty stage line horses get to it, you won't have a chance."

"Thank you, Tobias." Will grabbed a wooden pail and skimmed enough clear water off the top to shave and wash up. The barn usually served as shelter during inclement weather for coachmen and the team, but tonight, they would be sleeping outside wherever a breeze might be found.

Luke pulled the pin disconnecting the team from the stagecoach. A spot was chosen beyond the tables on the lawn. Will thought, *That's a strange place to leave a coach.* He would learn that it was left there to promote the new stagecoach of Smith and Jones Stage lines.

The stage line provided essentials for passengers at Chappell Hill who could not afford to stay in the inn overnight. Soap and a wash basin were behind a screen for privacy. There were two privies beyond the corral. A stone walkway provided easy access. Built-in bunks for up to eight people were in a room built onto the barn, but it would go unused tonight.

Will attempted to remove a few spots from his cleanest dirty shirt. What could not be removed was covered with a silk bandana hanging down from his neck. His thick handlebar moustache glistened with beeswax. He was ready to enjoy a good meal and be entertained by Miss Fontaine. Guests were beginning to arrive, dressed to the nines. They arrived in shiny new carriages driven by well-dressed Black men. The ladies wore elegant gowns like he had only seen in St. Louis and New Orleans. It was so unlike the Texas he knew. He felt underdressed, and he was.

Will asked, "Who are these people, Luke?"

"Rich cotton farmers from back east." Luke said as he looked up from the coach tack. "They bought land at a dollar an acre, brought their slaves, turned this blackland sod upside down. They are growing three thousand pounds of cotton an acre along the Yegua and the Brazos. Depending on the price of cotton, they are making one to three hundred dollars an acre. Except this year there may not be a cotton crop at all if it don't start raining soon."

Will thought about John Day. He'd had six hundred and forty acres of farmland on the Yegua Creek. *That boy is going to be rich if he learns to farm cotton.*

Tobias came out of the inn with a crisp white shirt and a tie on. He looked around the growing crowd. When he spotted Will and Luke, Tobias ran over to them, looking harried.

Will said, "Look at you, Tobias."

Tobias said, "Miss Fontaine sent me to find you. She wants you to come to her room."

Will was surprised and asked, "Now?"

Tobias said, "It must be important!"

"Why do you think it's so important, Tobias?"

"Because she gave me a whole silver dollar to find you." Tobias showed it to Will, then Luke. "See?"

Luke laughed and the usual stoic mail agent even feigned a grin.

Will said, "Let's go see what's so important, Tobias."

Tobias and Will went in through the servant's entrance. The pleasant smells of bread and pastries baking overwhelmed Will for a moment. It brought back fond memories of the kitchen of Angelina Eberly's Boarding House in Austin.

Everyone was busy preparing a feast for what Tobias said

were over a hundred people. Tobias took him to Miss Fontaine's room and knocked lightly.

Annie said, "Will, please come in."

Will motioned for Tobias to open the door and go in.

Tobias shook his head. "She called your name, not mine." Tobias bounced down the stairs to the kitchen. Will entered a room where Annie's undergarments were hanging everywhere. She sat at a dressing table in a silk bathrobe. She turned toward Will, revealing that the robe was all she had on. Will remained stoic while his mind went elsewhere.

Annie said, "Will, I need your help."

Will said, "I hope you don't need me to move that trunk for you!"

Annie laughed, "You're so funny. Can I trust you with a secret?"

Will said, "I'm sworn to uphold the law. If you have broken any law, please don't tell me."

Annie said, "No, silly boy, it's about my act." She picked up her fan. "Damn this heat. How do you stand it?"

"We get used to it. What do you want me to do?" Will looked at her a bit frustrated and hot in his own way.

"I want you to disappear."

Will turned, "I can do that."

"No, during my act, you silly Willy."

Annie explained how she could not afford an assistant to tour with her. She tried to find someone at each venue to perform a disappearing act from her large trunk. It was important that her assistant not reveal her secret.

Will said, "Tell me what I need to do."

Annie explained, "The trunk will be empty as it is now. It will be my last act of the evening. The host will call for the Sheriff of Starr County to come to the platform."

She opened the trunk and motioned for Will to get in. Once in, Annie gave the simple instructions for his escape. They tried the stunt twice and it worked well each time.

Annie said, "I must get ready to perform now." She opened the door and gave Will a kiss on the cheek.

Will went back down the stairs and through the kitchen. A very pregnant woman stopped Will in the kitchen and said, "Sheriff, I'm Mary Beth Haller, Jacob's wife. I want to thank you for bringing Titan home to us. Jacob has been so distraught over losing him—."

One of the servants asked her a question. She had to take care of a problem in the kitchen. An older woman came up to Will with a plate full of pastries.

"Sheriff, I'm Mary Beth's mother. This plate we made for you and the stagecoach people. I hope y'all enjoy the festivities."

"Thank you for the pastries!" Will said, as she hurried away.

It was showtime on the lawn of the Stagecoach Inn. Patrons had dined on the smorgasbord of food and had drunk the wine of the mustang grape. The ancient oak and pecan trees provided much-needed shade from the late afternoon sun. Fortunately, a gentle gulf breeze found its way to Chappell Hill.

Two hours of daylight remained when Jacob Haller stepped on the slightly elevated stage. He welcomed the guests and introduced the local dignitaries. Then the show began with the introduction of Anna Belle Fontaine. She wore a shiny red dress that fit her well. She sang and played a banjo to the music of Stephen Foster that included "Oh! Susanna" and "De Camptown Races." The crowd loved the songs of the old south.

After thirty minutes of music, Annie took a fifteen-minute break. Returning in the costume of a court jester, complete with a fool's cap, she juggled balls and plates without a fumble. The second act ended with her twisting and turning as a contortionist. She took her second break to come back dressed as a magician. She did several magic tricks using different props. Then the master of ceremonies, Jacob Haller, called for the Sheriff of Starr County to come up. On cue, Will was there.

Jacob Haller helped Annie stand the large trunk on end and open it to show the audience it was empty and had a solid bottom. Will stepped inside the trunk. She wrapped chains around it, then had someone from the audience lock the chains with a large padlock. She then distracted the audience by pulling a rabbit out of her top hat. She put the rabbit back in the hat, waved her magic wand, and the white dove flew out above the audience. Applause from the audience was Will's que to escape by the false bottom. The show earned a standing ovation and Will disappeared into the dark of night to spend some time alone with a horse he called Blue.

The next morning, Will sat on the coach step wiping down his dusty revolvers. The mail agent and Luke could be heard sparring. "I work for the U.S. Postal Service. Lugging this heavy luggage isn't my job!" the mail agent said.

"It isn't my job to keep your skinny ass from being scalped by the Indians, like our last trip to Galveston!" Luke set the trunk down in front of Will.

Will said, "Sounds like you boys need some help."

The mail agent nodded, and Luke said, "We could use your help!"

Annie stood behind them with her birdcage, waiting to get in the coach. Annie said, "Indians tried to scalp you?" looking at the mail clerk and Luke. Neither answered, as the stage line discouraged such talk.

Will said, "Good morning, Annie. Your show was the best solo performance I've ever seen."

Annie said, "Thank you, Will. You did your part well."

Luke asked, "Dammit, Will, you going to help us or not?"

Will said, "Hold your horses, Luke. Annie, what's the heaviest thing you have in your trunk?"

"I guess my weighted juggling pins and balls." Annie answered.

Will asked, "What would be the next heaviest?"

"My musical instruments, I suppose." Annie looked perplexed at the trunk.

Will asked, "Would you mind taking them out until we get the trunk on top of the stagecoach?"

Annie opened the trunk and removed nearly a hundred pounds of weight. The three men easily hoisted the trunk to the top of the coach. Then they placed the heavy items back neatly in the trunk.

Will assisted Annie and her menagerie into the stagecoach, then sat on the opposite seat. He looked at Annie and asked, "Opened or closed?"

Annie said, "Closed for now." She stifled a snicker, remembering yesterday's fiasco.

Luke shook the reins. The stage lurched forward, and they were on their way to Galveston by way of Houston. It was another hot August day. Annie suggested Will move to the back bench so he might catch some wind blowing in the side windows. He found it much more comfortable riding facing forward and removed his boots.

Annie asked Will the usual get-acquainted questions. "Are you married?"

When he said no, Annie asked, "Why not?"

Will said, "Why do women always ask if I am married?"

Annie said, "I can't answer for the other women, but for me I want to know if you are available or not. If you are not, I will turn my attention to my bird and my rabbit."

Will looked at her but didn't say anything until she began talking to her rabbit. He then began to tell her what she wanted to hear. He was traveling to Wilmington, Delaware on business. His family came to Texas, he became a Texas Ranger, then the Sheriff of Starr County. He told Annie about his lady friend in Rio Grande City.

Once Will told his story, Annie told the story of her French Huguenot grandparents fleeing France after the revolution. They'd arrived in Philadelphia and opened a restaurant and bakery. Her father entertained the customers with magic and juggling acts. He became a popular attraction at the Chestnut Street Theatre in Philadelphia.

Annie continued, "He met my mother, who was a dancer and contortionist there. I was born in the dressing room of the theater. I grew up in the theater. It's all I know! My parents, older brother, and I performed as a team in London, Paris, and aboard the ships as we traveled—."

Will asked, "Where are they?"

"I lost my family to cholera last year in Philadelphia. To survive, I created a one-person show doing everything myself that the four of us had done. This tour of Texas is my premier performance. We will see how it goes!" Annie shrugged her shoulders.

Will said, "I think you did great! Especially making that sheriff from Starr County disappear."

Annie snuggled close to Will. She was comfortable with him. The stage arrived at the Capitol Hotel in Houston. Annie offered Will the opportunity to be her traveling companion to Philadelphia via ship, which would leave the day after to-morrow from Galveston for New Orleans. She explained how it would be the fastest and most direct route to Wilmington, Delaware.

She performed her last act in Texas to a sold-out crowd of over a hundred in the ballroom of the Capitol Hotel. The Sheriff of Starr County disappeared again.

Chapter Twenty

Once aboard the *Columbia* at the Port of Galveston, Will reminisced about his first two trips on this vessel. The stateroom he shared with Annie was the same one he'd used on Easter weekend 1842. It was in this room the munitions were transported to Texas for the Vasquez Campaign.

Annie and Will were at sea for sixty-two hours. Then six more hours up the Mississippi River to the Port of New Orleans. They chose to stay overnight on the *Columbia* rather than lug Annie's trunk to a hotel, and they boarded the *Shenandoah* the next day. The 143-foot packet ship sailed back and forth from New Orleans to Philadelphia every other week. The trip was a week's journey in good weather.

While in New Orleans, Will wanted to exchange his DuPont check for bank notes. The Citizens' Bank of Louisiana was the oldest and most trusted bank in the city with sufficient assets to handle a large transaction. Will understood this bank also had a relationship with Farmers Bank of Delaware which the DuPont check was written on.

Annie needed bank notes exchanged for silver she received in tips and her share of the receipts. They entered the bank together.

The lobby was empty. Will looked for the manager, while Annie went straight to a teller window. Converting silver to bank notes could be done by any employee of the bank. Large out-of-town checks cashed for bank notes was a different matter. Fortunately, Will kept the envelope complete with red wax seal which was sufficient evidence that the payment came from the DuPont company. Will asked for one hundred dollars in silver and one hundred in bank notes. The funds remaining would be deposited into a new bank account in his name.

"We may not have a hundred dollars in silver. I'll check with the tellers." The manager went to the teller's cage and saw Annie pushing stacks of silver toward the teller. Perplexed at what he observed, the manager went to Mr. O'Brien, who was president of the bank.

The manager said, "A Mister 'Smith,' from Texas is at my desk with a large check from the DuPont company. He's asked for a large sum of silver and bank notes. I suspect this couple in the lobby are attempting to flimflam our bank."

Mr. O'Brien and the manager stepped out into the lobby, both suspecting the strangers were there to commit fraud. The manager introduced Will to the president of the bank and turned the transaction over to Mr. O'Brien. The president sat down in the manager's chair.

Mr. O'Brien said, "Thank you, Mr. Smith, for your confidence in our bank with such a large deposit from such an esteemed company as DuPont. What is your business with DuPont?" He looked closely at the check, then at Will.

Will said, "Bat shit."

Mr. O'Brien said, "I beg your pardon?"

Will said, "Bat shit. I sell them bat shit. You know, to make gunpowder." Will did not want to reveal his connection to DuPont or Mr. Bidermann, as it was none of the bank's business.

Mr. O'Brien said, "I prefer to personally handle large deposits such as yours. I understand you want one hundred dollars in silver and one hundred in bank notes. Our policy in situations like this is to receive the funds first from the Farmers Bank of Delaware before we advance any funds on a new account."

Will asked, "How long will it take to do that?"

Mr. O'Brien said, "If I can get it on today's packet ship to Philadelphia, it would be at least two weeks turnaround time."

Will said, "That won't work! We are sailing this afternoon to Philadelphia. I will just take care of it at the Farmers Bank of Delaware." Will stood to leave, which, to the bank president, was a clue that they were not there to commit fraud.

Mr. O'Brien stood and said, "You look familiar, Mr. Smith. I think we have met somewhere! Do you come to New Orleans often?"

Will said, "This is my third trip to New Orleans. Last time was about eight years ago."

Mr. O'Brien's attitude turned friendlier, and it was obvious he remembered Will. "Were you ever a Texas Ranger?"

Will said, "Yes, I was. I'm the Sheriff of Starr County now," thinking that he knew Mr. O'Brien from somewhere.

Mr. O'Brien stood up and walked around the desk with his arms out and said, "Mr. Smith, you saved me from a wretched woman on the wharf. It was the day after Easter. It's been eight years and I will never forget the moment you arrested her, as I was helping her onto the *Queen of Saint Louie.*"

He put his arms on Will's shoulders. "Thank you, Mr. Smith! At first, I assumed you were the villain, and she was the victim." He shook his head.

Will smiled and said, "And I thought you were her pimp, until I saw her pick your pockets."

Mr. O'Brien said, "It just goes to show you not to make

snap decisions about a person." He glanced at his bank manager. "Days later, I read in the *Picayune* how she stabbed you in the back shortly after I left the scene. Witnesses said as you lay on the pier bleeding from your wounds, she tried to stab you again in the heart. You pulled a derringer just in time, killing her in self-defense." Mr. O'Brien pulled his gold pocket watch out of his vest pocket and showed it to Will. "Thanks to you, I still have my watch and wallet. I'm glad you survived your injuries and you're still a man of the law."

Annie had made her way to the two men and heard the last half of their conversation. Will saw her look of shock. He knew Annie would insist on hearing the whole story. A story that he had never told anyone before.

Will received his silver, bank notes, and a handful of Mr. O'Brien's best cigars. The bank teller drove them first to the French Market, where Annie purchased fruits, vegetables, and baked goods for the voyage. Then straight to the wharf for boarding. The trunk and bird cage were on the dock waiting to be transferred to the *Shenandoah*. Annie was upset the trunk and her precious bird and rabbit had been left unattended on the dock, and let the ship's first mate know she did not appreciate it!

They boarded the *Shenandoah*, and Will paid the additional passenger fee. They checked out their stateroom, which was too small for Annie's trunk. On the forward deck they found a bench to sit on and ate their fresh beignets from the French Market. They watched the trunk brought aboard to be stored in the steerage compartment below the main deck.

Will said, "You sure keep a close eye on that magic trunk."

Annie said, "Yes, it's a magic trunk. Without it, I have no show, and no show means no dough!"

Will grinned. "Clever, Annie. I've never seen one like it;

where did you find such a trunk?"

"My father found a trunk maker in London on our first tour. The gold crest on the front is the Fontaine family crest. The vignettes etched into the corners are sketches of our family. Wherever we performed, the trunk was with us. It felt like home."

They watched other passengers board the *Shenandoah*. Those who could not afford a cabin would endure at least seven days of close quarters with two hundred strangers in the steerage compartment. Will felt most fortunate to share a stateroom with Annie.

The ship's three masts were at the ready as the crew worked their way into the Mississippi ship channel by steam. Somewhere south of the New Orleans wharf was where Will's father, Thomas W. Smith, Sr., fought the British with the Tennessee Militia during the War of 1812. Will wondered how the mountain men of Tennessee could have beaten back the world's greatest army in a swamp such as this.

It was dark when the *Shenandoah* reached the gulf. Will and Annie ate early and lightly in preparation for the ocean's swells that were to come. Will had sailed the gulf without sea sickness on three occasions. Annie warned Will that the month of August was the middle of hurricane season. Before retiring for the evening, Annie wanted to check on the trunk. They searched the fore and aft cargo holds and could not find her trunk. They found the captain on the bridge and asked where the trunk was.

The captain explained, "We have stored your oversized trunk aft on the port side. It was too bulky to stow below decks. Your trunk is secured and covered in tarpaulin. Rest assured, your luggage will be safe where it is."

Annie looked stricken. "It's not luggage…it's my everything.

It shouldn't be stored outside."

"Then you should have registered it and insured it as such!" The captain admonished Annie and asked them to leave the bridge. Annie was in tears as they worked their way to the aft deck. She recognized the size and shape of her trunk. Will pulled up about six inches of the tarp for Annie to see it.

On the third night at sea shortly after midnight, the helmsman of the *Shenandoah* spotted what looked like a tropical storm between the Islands of Key West and Cuba. The storm produced heavy thunder and lightning, making it visible from afar. The captain was advised that it appeared to be dead ahead, traveling toward the southern coast of Florida. He ordered the sails dropped and steam power reduced to two knots, enough speed to slowly maneuver away from the storm toward Havana, Cuba. The nautical diversion cost a few hours of travel time but resulted in no damage to the ship or its cargo.

Once into the Florida Straits, the warm Gulf Stream currents helped to push the *Shenandoah* toward its destination. Unfortunately, the same tropical storm the captain avoided was now crossing the State of Florida and gaining in strength. Ominous dark clouds approached the coastline near where the St. Lucia River flowed into the Atlantic Ocean.

It was dark as Will and Annie scurried to the aft deck of the ship to check on the trunk. All tiedowns were secure and the tarp was snug.

Annie asked, "Will, what if the lines don't hold?"

Will said, "We have done all that can be done. The lines are in good shape and properly tied. Everything is now in God's hands."

A gigantic bolt of lightning struck close by, illuminating the ship's deck. Large drops of rain began to fall as another lightning bolt lit up the sky. Will and Annie worked their way back to the cabin. A crewman told them to keep their life rings at the ready, which gave Annie and Will little comfort. They tied the bird cage from a hook in the ceiling. The bird and rabbit stayed calm as Will and Annie were tossed from one side of the room to the other for nearly two hours. Once the storm clouds moved out to sea toward Bermuda, the swells ceased, the sea was calmer, and the ship picked up speed. Will checked on Annie's trunk and found it secure. All passengers and crew on the *Shenandoah* were accounted for.

They arrived in Philadelphia in the afternoon on Monday, the second day of September 1850. Annie was excited to show Will her home on North Water Street. He would be her first guest in the home her grandparents built, the only home she had ever known. But when the ship slowly passed the Vine Street Wharf on the Delaware River, the wharf and warehouses were not there. Four blocks of North Water Street were void of any structures.

Annie cried, "It's gone! The whole neighborhood is gone! My home is not there anymore. It was right there." She pointed. "When I left in March, my friends and neighbors lived and worked here. What happened, Will?" She reached out to Will. He hugged her tightly but could not find words to comfort her.

They learned that on the ninth day of July, there'd been a large explosion that killed twenty-eight people and injured hundreds more. The fire that followed destroyed hundreds of warehouses and homes. Most of the ruins had been pushed off into the river. All Annie had left was her bird, a rabbit, and what was in her trunk.

Philadelphia was where Will's great grandparents arrived in

the eighteenth century. He thought, *It may have been near here! Annie's family may have known them.*

They chose the Girard House hotel to stay in as it was close to the Chestnut Street Theatre where Annie would be performing for a week. They hired two teamsters to take them to the hotel. On the way, they stopped at where Annie's home once was. The scarred remains of the foundation were evidence of the intensity of the heat that destroyed her home. Annie asked to be left alone to grieve the loss of the only home she had ever known. She sat on a rock step that was once the first step to the front porch. She cried as Will and the teamsters walked around the ruins.

When Annie looked like she was ready to leave, Will said, "Let's see if this Girard House has a room big enough for your trunk."

Annie said, "Thank you, Will, for being here." They walked slowly to the wagon. Annie rode in the bed of the wagon, sitting on a stool next to her trunk. Will rode on the buckboard with the driver. His young helper rode on the tailgate, his feet dangling beneath him. Will looked at the sights and listened to the sounds of a busy city. Over three hundred thousand people now called Philadelphia home. Will thought, *That is one hundred thousand more two-legged critters than Texas has in the entire state!*

Will was impressed with the size of Philadelphia but only desired to be a visitor for as long it took to help Annie find a home and take care of business. Will had read about and looked forward to sending a telegraph from Philadelphia to Mr. Bidermann in Wilmington. Once Annie was settled into the hotel, Will walked to the new Washington Telegraph Company office. He stood in line to send a telegraph to Mr. Bidermann at DuPont headquarters in Wilmington, Delaware.

He overheard the clerk telling someone to keep the message short and simple. Will used a short wooden pencil provided at the counter to complete his first telegraph order. He printed his message one letter at a time, using only eight of the twenty boxes on the form. He penciled the message, "Will from TX." stop. "I'm in Phil." stop. "Awaiting reply." stop. He paid two bits for the telegram and took a seat in the lobby to wait, proud that he had used this modern communication device that had yet to reach Texas. He envisioned how the telegraph could be used to warn the small Texas towns about Indian attacks and outlaw raids.

Shortly the manager came into the lobby and called out, "Will Smith!"

Will said, "That's me!"

The manager said, "Glad to meet you, Mr. Smith. Please follow me."

As they walked to the back of the long but narrow building, the telegraph company manager explained that the DuPont company had made a considerable investment in establishing the local telegraph company. They were the first customer to have their own teletype machine and morse code operator. Will's telegraph would be the first to go directly to DuPont's offices in Wilmington, Delaware from the Philadelphia station, thirty miles away.

The station manager said, "Make yourself comfortable while I send your wire. We should hear something soon."

In short time, the teletype started its clicking noise. The manager listened closely to the code of Samuel Morse which had been patented only two years before. Every employee regardless of their position was required to know Morse Code.

The manager wrote the words on the telegraph pad and tore it off for Will.

The message said, "Phil Hotel, solo tonight 1800."

Will was a bit confused and asked, "What does that mean?"

The manager said, "I believe Mr. Bidermann is saying he will meet you tonight at the Philadelphian Hotel at six and to come alone. Do you wish to confirm the appointment?"

Will asked, "What should I say?"

"'Confirmed' is all you need to say in your reply. Brevity is the key to telegraphic communication." The manager handed him a sheet of tips and suggestions on communicating by telegraph. "You'll learn. Take this, it may help you. I know it's strange to you now. There are presently twelve thousand miles of telegraph lines in operation. In time, every business in the United States will have telegraph service."

Will raised his eyebrows. "You think so?"

The manager nodded and opened the door for Will. "When you need to send a telegram, Mr. Smith, ask for me; James Donovan is my name. Whatever your business is with Mr. B., I know it is important. Whatever your real name is, I shall call you Mr. S. from Texas."

Will said, "Thank you for your help and for your information. My name is Will Smith and I'm really from Texas!"

The manager said, "Certainly you are, Mr. Smith." He winked. "Have a good day!"

Chapter Twenty-One

Will arrived back at their room at the Girard House to find the white dove perched on a window valance. The rabbit scampered around, looking for the bird. Will didn't see Annie at first. When he did, he fell back on the bed laughing and said, "What the hell?"

"I'm doing yoga! Haven't you ever seen anyone doing yoga before?"

"I don't know about yoga! But no, I've never seen a body twisted to where their head is between their thighs. I thought you were an end table for a moment. It's a wonder I didn't place my hat on you."

Annie laughed, knowing she looked awkward. She started walking in that position and Will came off the bed still laughing. "You look like one of those big pink birds walking in the swamp we saw going down the Mississippi River."

"Like a flamingo?" Annie animated her arms like a flamingo walking.

Will laughed louder. "Yes, that's it. A flamingo in the swamp."

"Are you making fun of me?" Annie straightened herself up into a human position.

Will said, "You're the best contortionist I've ever seen!"

Annie smiled, "I'm the only contortionist you've ever seen."

"But you're still the best *I* have ever seen!" Will and Annie laughed together.

They hugged. Will said, "I'm glad you can still laugh, Annie. I just don't know when or how to say comforting words."

Annie said, "I know you care; that's why I like you." She shoved Will onto the bed and climbed on top of him.

After some rigorous lovemaking with acrobatic moves that Will had never encountered, Annie collapsed on top of him.

Will said, "Annie, I have an important meeting at the Philadelphian Hotel at six. How long will it take me to get there?"

Annie said, "You need to leave now, Will! Why didn't you tell me? My family and I performed there many times. I will go and show you around."

"The businessman I am meeting specifically asked that I come alone." Will handed the telegram to Annie who read it. "You're meeting Antoine Bidermann?"

Will asked, "Yes, is there something I should know?"

"You must hurry. Please give Antoine and Evelina my regards."

Will headed out the door. He found a carriage waiting for a fare. "I can't be late!" he told the driver.

"Where to?" the carriage driver asked.

Will said, "The Philadelphian. Get me there by six and I'll double your fare."

The driver let out a whistle and popped his whip over the lead horse's head. Both horses responded in unison. Will held on to his hat as the carriage raced down the cobblestone streets of Philadelphia.

As they approached the Philadelphian, Will recognized the waiting carriage with the du Pont crest on the door. He knew Mr. Bidermann was there. He gave his driver two dollars in silver, and they were both happy. Will headed for the hotel's front entrance. Someone whistled. Then he heard "Mr. Smith! Over here." It was the driver of the coach. Two armed guards motioned him over. The larger guard said, "Mr. Smith, Mr. B. is waiting for you in the carriage."

The other guard asked, "Are you armed?"

Will said, "Certainly I'm armed. My derringer is in my right boot."

The guard said, "I will need it before you get in with Mr. B."

A voice inside the coach said, "Let him keep his derringer." The door opened and it was Mr. Bidermann. He said, "Get in, Will, we'll take a ride along the Delaware." The bodyguard disguised as a footman closed the door.

Will said, "Thank you for meeting with me so promptly, Mr. Bidermann."

Mr. Bidermann said, "The pleasure is mine. It's been nine years since we said goodbye in New Orleans."

After an exchange of pleasantries, Mr. Bidermann asked, "What brings you to Philadelphia?" He knew full well why Will was there.

Will said, "I'm here to thank you for the generous payment and letter you recently sent to Austin. I deposited the note in the Citizens' Bank of Louisiana in New Orleans."

Mr. Bidermann said, "It's a good bank. If you like, I can arrange to have future commissions sent there."

Will said, "I would appreciate that." Will pulled out the requisition list of supplies and ammunition from Governor Bell. "Can you fill this order and extend credit to Texas as you have in the past?"

Mr. Bidermann studied the list, doing calculations in his head. "Then it's true that Governor Bell intends to invade Santa Fe?"

Will said, "The governor has requested funding from the

legislature for three thousand troops and the munitions on that list."

Mr. Bidermann said, "As you've been traveling Will, you aren't aware of what has transpired in the last week. I received word today that the Texas House of Representatives on the twenty-sixth day of August approved appropriations for twenty-five hundred militiamen and this arsenal." Bidermann flicked the munitions list with his finger. "You understand this border dispute between Texas and New Mexico could lead to a civil war?"

Will said, "How so? It's a simple boundary dispute!"

Mr. Bidermann said, "No, it's not simple, it's quite complicated. The Texas border dispute is attached to an omnibus bill created by Senator Henry Clay of Kentucky. Three of the issues are a compromise about slavery, one is about California statehood. Then there is the issue of the Texas-New Mexico border. New Mexico wants to come into the Union as a free state and Texas wants to stay a slave state. New Mexico considers Santa Fe and Worth Counties within its territory."

Will said, "What you're trying to say is, our border dispute is about slavery?"

Mr. Bidermann answered, "Yes, but in a roundabout way. Legislation is like making gunpowder. You must add a lot of smelly bat shit to make your powder burn. Gunpowder is not pretty to watch being made. Neither is legislation. What is important to a shopkeeper in Pennsylvania may mean little to a rancher in Texas. That's why Senator Clay has suggested this five-part compromise. It's not a perfect meal, but it may satisfy the pallet enough to avoid a civil war."

Will said, "So, you're saying that to settle our boundary issues, Congress must accept California as a free state, allow New Mexico and Utah to come in as they wish, then abolish slavery in Washington, D.C.?"

Mr. Bidermann nodded. "It's the slavery issue that has muddled up your boundary dispute. Mississippi's governor has warned the president that if federal troops try to intervene against Texas, Mississippi will send troops to aid Texas. Then other slave states will join in the fight. The slave states will secede as they have been threatening to do. Then we have a civil war!"

Will shook his head. "Where did you hear that?"

"In today's paper. I also read how young men from all over Texas are showing up on the capitol steps in Austin to enlist."

Will asked, "Mr. Bidermann, when can we get that order shipped to Galveston?"

"I can get everything but the gunpowder out this week. We have less than a ton of gunpowder in inventory." Mr. Bidermann shook his head. "That's all we have at the moment. It might be months before we can start production again."

"I don't understand. Gunpowder is the backbone of your business!"

"Yes, it has been, but we have encountered a problem." Mr. Bidermann beat on the roof of the carriage and it stopped. Bidermann called out to the driver, "James, take us to the ruins of our warehouse. I want to show Mr. Smith why we're out of business."

When they stopped, Will realized it was very near where Annie's house had been before the explosion. Mr. Bidermann explained that on the day President Zachary Taylor died, DuPont 's warehouses of saltpeter were destroyed, along with hundreds of homes in the neighborhood. The step that Annie sat on and cried earlier that day was only one hundred feet from where they stood.

Will's mind raced trying to comprehend what Bidermann

was about to say without letting on that he already knew what had happened. Until now, Will had no idea that DuPont was involved. Bidermann implied he thought it was intentionally set by someone who knew they were storing saltpeter on the wharf.

Mr. Bidermann continued, "Fire officials say a spark of some kind ignited hay in a nearby stable which set fire to the roof of our warehouse. When the heated saltpeter ignited, twenty tons of bat guano lit up the harbor, destroying hundreds of homes, killing many and injuring hundreds. This was the biggest fire in the history of Philadelphia. That's why I don't know when we can fill your order."

Will asked, "You were manufacturing gunpowder here?"

Mr. Bidermann responded, "No, that would be too dangerous in the city. We only stored the saltpeter in the warehouse. Then flatboated it down the Delaware as needed for production. Saltpeter alone is not combustible, that is why I suspect arson. In the meanwhile, Pennsylvania has prohibited us from rebuilding our warehouse in any incorporated city in the state. We have no saltpeter and without it, there is no gunpowder."

Will said, "Ship Texas what you have and the rest when you get it produced."

Mr. Bidermann said, "I can send a hundred five-pound kegs now. That will fire about thirty thousand rounds."

Will said, "That's only twelve rounds per man."

Mr. Bidermann showed Will his open hands. "It's all I have, Will."

Will shook his head. "They'll use that much ammunition shooting rattlesnakes."

Mr. Bidermann said, "Let's pray Henry Clay's compromise is approved, and no blood will be shed! Remember—only you and I know DuPont has no black powder to furnish an army."

They walked toward the carriage.

Will asked, "This mission Governor Bell has sent me on... the whole damn thing about war between Texas and the Union is just a bluff, isn't it?"

Mr. Bidermann said, "If it is, Will, you and Texas hold the ace!"

Will asked, "What cards do *you* hold, Mr. Bidermann?"

"I'm just the dealer!" They climbed into the carriage "Like poker. Either way, I win. When we have inventory, Texas, Mississippi, and the Union's orders will be shipped."

Will said, "If Henry Clay's compromise settles the issues, there will be no war and the munitions will not be needed."

Mr. Bidermann said, "As long as men have weapons, there will be a need for an arsenal."

Mr. Bidermann offered to take Will to his hotel. As they rode along the devastation of Vine Street, the only sound was the clip-clop of horses' hooves on the street. At the Girard House, Annie had a view of the street below and recognized the familiar du Pont carriage. She brushed her hair and wrapped a shawl over her shoulders and proceeded down the stairs just as Will stepped out of the carriage. Annie said, "Will, I have been so worried about you!"

Mr. Bidermann leaned out and asked, "Is that Annie Fontaine, back from her Texas tour?"

"Yes, it is, Mr. Bidermann. It is so good to see you again. I see you've met my friend Will, who I found in Texas."

Mr. Bidermann climbed down from the carriage, bowed his head and kissed Annie's hand. "Evelina will be so excited to know you are back." Mr. Bidermann looked at Will and asked, "Are you aware how talented this young lady is?"

Will nodded and smiled at Annie, "I am aware of her many talents!" She gave Will a mischievous smile and a quick wink that Mr. Bidermann noticed.

Mr. Bidermann said, "Annie, seeing as you and Will know each other so well, why don't you both come to our new home for dinner tomorrow evening? Plan to spend the night. My carriage will pick you up at two and return you the following day."

"We look forward to it," Will and Annie said in unison as Mr. Bidermann stepped up into his carriage. Once the carriage had pulled away, they embraced passionately on the steps of the Girard House. The doorman cleared his throat, alerting the couple of his presence and holding the door for them.

Annie giggled excitedly as she hurriedly led Will up the stairs to their room. Once the door was shut and locked, Will said, "I assume we're not going out to dinner tonight!"

Chapter Twenty-Two

The next day, Tuesday, September the third, a shiny carriage arrived at the Girard House a quarter before two. The ornate carriage belonged to Madame Evelina du Pont-Bidermann. It was driven by her personal coachman, assisted by a footman. Will and Annie waited anxiously in the lobby with their bags. When the footman reached for Will's bag, which contained his matching colt revolvers, Will said, "Don't touch my bag!"

The coachman told the footman in French. "He is a Texan. Do what he says!" The nervous footman carried Annie's bag and followed them out to the open carriage.

The thirty-mile ride along the Delaware River would take several hours. Two French Trotters, bred on the du Pont farm, moved the carriage swiftly in perfect cadence.

Annie smiled at Will as she secured her bonnet with a piece of yellow ribbon. "You know you scared the footman, don't you? I heard them say something in French about you nearly shooting du Pont's manservant for taking your guns. Is that true?"

Will said, "Maybe...I don't recall." He wrapped an arm around Annie. She settled comfortably into his arms.

Will asked, "So you have been to the Bidermann's home?"

Annie said, "Only to entertain their guests. This is the first time I have been invited as their guest for dinner. I'm excited! Aren't you, Will?"

Will said, "No, not excited. Curious, I guess, to see how the richest family in the world lives."

"Does anything ever impress you?" Annie looked at Will for an answer.

Will thought for a moment and said, "When I was eighteen years old, the day my family reached the Sabine River, we reached a high point looking down on the river. I saw Texas for the first time. Hundreds of buffalo grazing in the lush grass of the river valley. That impressed me!" Will nodded his head.

Annie shook her head and looked back at Will, "How long have you known Mr. Bidermann?"

Will said, "It was nine years ago we met at Council Grove on the Santa Fe Trail. Bidermann and du Pont traveled with me to New Orleans."

Annie said, "You're old friends then, with Bidermann and du Pont."

Will said, "Not really. My time with them has always been about business. I actually know very little about either of them. Du Pont is a little strange, but both have been good to me."

Annie said, "Antoine's wife is Evelina Gabriella du Pont-Bidermann. Her father was Éleuthère Irénée du Pont who founded the DuPont company. Her brother is Alfred Victor du Pont who everyone simply calls DuPont. Alfred is still the president, but Antoine runs the business and has a vast interest in it. No one knows what has happened to Alfred."

Will said, "It was Alfred du Pont who introduced me to Bidermann."

Annie asked, "What is your business with Mr. Bidermann?"

"I'm sorry, Annie, I can't discuss anything about that. I'm surprised he invited us, and I ask that you not ask him any questions about our business, unless Bidermann brings it up."

Annie said, "You are so secretive. I know absolutely nothing about you! Other than you're the Sheriff of Starr County, Texas and a great lover!"

"For now, that will have to do!" Will glanced toward the coachman and his assistant, hoping they were not listening. Will knew that was not what Annie wanted to hear. He yearned to tell her more, but he could not jeopardize his mission.

A flight of Canada geese flying over the river changed the subject. "Look Will! Honkers!" Annie pointed toward hundreds of geese forming a giant V formation in the sky.

Will thought, *Those damn geese will be back in Texas before me.*

The carriage stopped at the sentry gate of the du Pont estate. After some discussion in French, they were waved through. The estate's northeast border was the Brandywine River, which separated Pennsylvania from Delaware. The coachman and footman assisted Annie out of the carriage. Will exited the opposite side of the carriage, hastily grabbing their bags. The Bidermanns and their staff of house servants stood at the entrance to Winterthur to welcome their guests. The butler stepped toward Will to relieve him of his bags.

Mr. Bidermann intervened. "Charles, you know our guest is from Texas, where men carry their own baggage." Slightly embarrassed, Charles realized it was Will, the Texas Ranger they'd encountered on the Santa Fe Trail in 1841. Will set down Annie's bag in front of Charles and held on to his own bag.

Mr. Bidermann introduced his wife Evelina, then the staff members. Will soon recognized Charles as the manservant of

Alfred du Pont, whom he'd met at Council Grove all those years ago.

Annie and Will were shown separate but adjoining rooms on the third floor, overlooking the sixty-acre garden. Winterthur was one of many homes on the twelve-hundred-acre estate. It was named for Mr. Bidermann's ancestorial home in Winterthur, Switzerland. Construction had begun on the three-story French Château in 1839. The Bidermanns now occupied it with their servants.

Annie opened the adjoining door to find Will with his shirt off. "What do you think of Winterthur?" she asked as she pushed Will down onto a lush featherbed with freshly pressed cotton linen.

Will said, "This is nice."

Annie said, "I like the smell of fresh linen."

Will said, "I like the smell of you!" He rolled on top of Annie, kissing her neck, which culminated in a torrent of mattress thrashing. A knock on the door from Mr. Bidermann's secretary interrupted their lovemaking. The well-dressed young man said, "Mr. Smith, I'm sorry to disturb you. You have visitors from Washington who've just arrived. They are waiting in Mr. Bidermann's office. They said it was urgent that they speak to you. Meet me in the foyer as soon as you can get dressed. I will take you to them. Mr. Bidermann asks that you come alone."

Will shut the door. "What's that about?" a disheveled Annie asked.

Will said, "I don't know, but I best hurry." He put on his suit, thinking, *I don't know anyone in Washington, D.C. They must be from Washington-on-the-Brazos. God, I hope nothing has happened to my family.*

Will entered Bidermann's smoke-filled office where three men sat smoking cigars. Mr. Bidermann rose to introduce them. Sam Houston, the U.S. Senator and twice President of Texas, stood to give Will the handshake of a Mason. Will received the same greeting from Thomas Rusk. Will knew who Senator Rusk was but had never met him.

Mr. Bidermann said, "Will, they came from Washington to see you! I will leave you Texans alone to discuss your business. As I said before, I would be honored if the two senators from Texas would stay for our dinner party."

Senator Houston stood again. "Thank you for asking, Mr. Bidermann. It's important that no one knows we were here! Besides, Senator Rusk and I must get back to Washington tonight. We meet with President Fillmore tomorrow. He wants us to give up sixty-seven million acres of Tex—"

Senator Rusk awkwardly interrupted Houston in a stutter, "Er, we will take you up...on that box of food...and a pint of your peach brandy."

Senator Houston said, "No brandy for me! I gave up all alcohol when I married Margaret Lea!"

Mr. Bidermann nodded. "Everything will be placed in your carriage. I hope you have a safe trip."

Mr. Bidermann turned to Will. "Please join us in the dining room after your meeting. I'll explain that you have been delayed. Evelina plans to take Annie on a tour of Winterthur before the other guests arrive."

Bidermann closed the door. Now Will was alone with the senators. One he hated, the other he'd just met. Both had signed the Texas Declaration of Independence from Mexico and led the attack on Santa Anna at San Jacinto.

Houston, now seated, motioned for Will to move closer. Will scooted his chair forward. Houston said, "Rusk, make sure no one is listening in the hallway."

Rusk moved to the door, opening it just enough to peek out both ways. He glanced at Houston and nodded.

Houston spoke in a whisper. "Will, this meeting never took place! Do you understand?"

Will nodded that he understood.

Houston said, "We understand that you have a requisition for materials of war from Governor Bell to be delivered by DuPont."

Will looked at Senator Houston suspiciously, not sure what to say as he didn't trust him. Will remained stoic and silent.

Rusk said, "Will, we received a communique from Governor Bell advising us that you were on your way from Texas to Wilmington with a requisition for ammunition."

Will sat tight-lipped in his chair. Rusk cleared his throat, something he did when he thought he was being ignored. He waited for an answer when it didn't come. Rusk looked at Houston for support and direction. Houston impatiently whisked his hand like shooing a fly toward Will. "Dammit! Just show Will the governor's letter!"

Rusk stuttered, "It's...supposed to be a confidential document."

"I know that!" Houston slapped his knee. "Governor Bell has most likely sworn Will to secrecy. You're wasting daylight! Just get on with it. Show Will the damn letter! He knows as much as we do about this situation."

Rusk was the senior senator from Texas. He usually acquiesced to Houston, who had been his commanding officer in the fight for Texas Independence.

Will read the correspondence, which was a weekly update on the affairs of Texas. It included the Texas Legislature's approval to enlist twenty-five hundred troops and the requisition to arm them for war against the people of New Mexico.

Rusk said, "The governor keeps us well informed on the happenings back in Texas. We received this timely piece of information this morning. After Houston and I read it, we immediately sent a wire to Bidermann, asking if you had been in contact with him. He replied that you would be here this evening. That is why we are here—to ask for your help!"

Will asked, "*My* help? What can I do for the most influential men in Texas?"

Houston explained, "We know Governor Bell has sworn you to secrecy about the munitions order he gave you as the agent for DuPont. Things have changed, Will. This so-called compromise has us on the horns of a dilemma. The issue for all states but Texas is slavery. I am strongly against slavery, but for Texas it's about sixty-seven million acres of land."

Houston continued, "I know the sacrifices you and your family made moving to Texas. Your father and I didn't always see eye to eye on things. However, we always did what we thought was right at the time. Your father and brother, James, wanted the capitol relocated from Houston. Now we know moving the capitol to Austin was a huge mistake."

Will puffed up a bit. "Why would you say that?"

Houston said, "Will, everyone knows removing the capitol from Houston was a mistake! That's why they jokingly call Austin 'Waterloo'. President Lamar's middle name is Bonaparte. Don't you get it?" Houston slapped his knee. "Austin was Lamar's Waterloo! Like Napoléon Bonaparte's loss."

Nine years of pent-up anger spilled out of Will's mouth as he stood up. "No, I don't get it and I never heard anyone in my presence ever call Austin 'Waterloo'."

The senators were dumfounded by Will's outburst. They motioned for him to sit down and lower his voice, which only incensed Will more. He walked to an open window that looked down on the garden. He took a deep breath of fresh air and tried to expel a decade of hatred for Houston. The senators were flabbergasted. Will regained his composure, turned, and spoke coherently, "Did either of you have anything to do with killing my brother and father!?"

Both senators were stunned by Will's question. They were unaware that the citizens of Austin suspected Sam Houston and his ilk of being instigators of Indian attacks on the capital city. Will wanted to use his well-honed interrogation skills to get answers to the questions that had haunted him since the murder of his brother James. Will's family reckoned the same Houston instigators planned the death of their father, Thomas W. Smith, too.

Houston looked stormy and asked, "Why would you think I would do such a thing? I respected your father and adored your mother, Rebeckah. While the legislature was in session, I spent many an evening on Angelina Eberly's front porch visiting with your family while you were away searching for Fayette."

Sam Houston had boarded at the Eberly Boarding House next door to Will's brother-in-law, Lorenzo Van Cleve. The Smith cabin and the courthouse were only a block away.

Will clenched his fist. "You never wanted the capitol to leave Houston, because it was named for you! You used their deaths and Fayette's abduction to scare people away. Once Austin dwindled to only a few families, you sent a convoy to Austin to steal the archives in the dead of night. If Mrs. Eberly had not caught your men in the act of removing the archives, you would have gotten away with it."

Senator Houston said, "I wasn't aware anyone thought I had something to do with the Indian attacks on your family."

Will said, "Everyone knows you were friendly with the Comanches. You gave the lands of Comancheria to them. And I know about your living with Indians before coming to Texas."

Houston said, "My point of view was published in the *Texas State Gazette*. I feared for those living in Austin with Buffalo Hump on the rampage. Yes, I warned everyone to leave Austin while they could."

Senator Rusk added, "It was fear of the Mexican Army and the Indians that scared everyone away from Austin."

Will pointed at Houston. "Then how would you have known that it was Buffalo Hump that killed my brother James?"

"That's what Sheriff Barton told me!" Houston thumped his walking stick hard on the wooden floor. "Will, we must get on with this important business. Texas needs your help! What must I do to convince you that I had nothing to do with the Indian depravations in Austin?"

The large Masonic ring on Houston's finger gave Will an idea. He paused for a moment, then looked at Rusk, who wore the same ring.

"I want you both to look me in the eye and swear on the oath of a Mason that you had nothing to do with their deaths."

Houston looked Will in the eye and said, "I swear on the oath of a Mason that I had nothing to do with the deaths of James and Thomas Smith or the kidnapping of Fayette Smith."

Rusk said, "Neither did I have anything to do with the attacks on your family."

Will sat down and sucked in a couple of breaths. He glanced at Houston, then at Rusk. He bit his lip and thought for a minute. "That's good! I am glad to hear you say that."

Houston said, "I ask that you tell your family I had nothing to do with the attacks."

Will said, "I can do that."

Houston explained that the U.S. Congress had offered Texas ten million dollars for sixty-seven million acres of its disputed land. Texas legislators and Governor Bell balked at the less-than-fifteen-cents-per-acre offer.

Senator Rusk said, "Senator Houston and I suggested that in addition to the ten million dollars offered that the federal government assume Texas's debt, which is more than we can ever repay."

Senator Houston shifted in his chair. "Since most of Texas debtholders are northerners, they are concerned about repayment, as Texas is in arrears on most of its obligations to them."

Will smirked. "Like our host, Mr. Bidermann?" Will shook his head, knowing that Mr. Bidermann had made that suggestion.

Senator Houston said, "Yes, Will, and Mr. Bidermann has many influential friends who will encourage their legislators and President Fillmore to pass this last hurdle of the Compromise of 1850."

Will asked, "What could I possibly do to help you?"

Houston reached into his coat pocket and retrieved a completed telegram form. The form had the DuPont emblem printed on it.

Will asked, "What's this?" Looking at the familiar DuPont imprint, he realized what it was and that it came from Bidermann's desk. It was a message to Texas Governor Bell from Will Smith, Texas agent for DuPont. It read: *Order shipped today from Phil on two vessels. Gather your troops.*

Will raised his eyebrows and looked at Senator Houston.

Houston said, "It must be sent from the Philadelphia telegraph station by you! As soon as they open. Make sure the stationmaster, a man named James Donovan, sends it."

Will said, "Senator Houston, I'm sworn—"

Senator Houston interrupted Will. "We understand you are sworn to secrecy." Houston placed both hands on top of his walking stick. "If the U.S. Congress hears a load of DuPont munitions is headed from Philadelphia to Texas, they will know Texas and the southern slave states are prepared for war."

Senator Rusk quickly added, "Will, no one wants a civil war. This compromise we have worked on for a year could be settled this week if members of congress thought Governor Bell was about to invade New Mexico Territory."

Senator Houston said, "That telegram from you can make that happen."

Will looked at the telegram in his hand. "This sounds like skullduggery to me!"

Houston said, "Yes, it is, Will. I pray it will work for us." Rusk nodded in agreement.

It was agreed. Will would board a well-marked DuPont keelboat loaded with nothing but sand. An unmarked clipper ship with the munitions would leave one hour later.

Chapter Twenty-Three

essert was being served when Will finally entered the dining room. Annie had been concerned about his absence. They were the guests of honor, and everyone was excited to meet the Sheriff of Starr County Texas. Especially Whig Congressman John W. Houston, who was the only U.S. Representative of the State of Delaware and no relation to Senator Sam Houston.

Mr. Bidermann introduced Will to the five couples around the long table. Will was embarrassed and apologized for his tardiness. He enjoyed the lamb chops and potatoes while the others enjoyed a crème brûlée with a snifter of cognac.

Representative John Houston asked, "Will, what are your thoughts about the ten million dollars offered from the federal government for the disputed lands of Texas?"

"It's a good down payment!" Will smiled.

Representative Houston said, "Ten million is a lot of money!"

Will countered, "Sixty-seven million acres is a lot of land!" He looked around the table and added, "Many brave Texans fought and died for it. It would be sad to see such hallowed ground sold for pennies an acre."

Mr. Bidermann clinked his water glass with a spoon for attention and to stop the talk of politics. Bidermann was the most knowledgeable person at the table when it came to politics, yet he and Evelina never allowed politics to be discussed at their dinner table.

Mr. Bidermann announced, "We have a delightful surprise for our guests. Anna Belle Fontaine, whom we all know as Annie, has graciously offered to sing a song or two for us tonight."

Annie sang two popular songs from her repertoire. Then she announced that her last song was dedicated to her homeless friends and neighbors who had lost everything in the recent Vine Street explosion and fire.

The song Annie chose to sing was "Ave Maria." She sang the ending in Latin. By the last note, nary an eye was dry and the room was devoid of any sound or movement.

Mr. Bidermann cleared his throat and slowly rose from his chair. He began to clap, and the guests followed his lead. Evelina nodded toward her servants. They began to clap in appreciation for Annie's performance. Annie curtsied.

Mr. Bidermann asked, "Annie, was your home near the wharf?"

Annie responded, "Yes, I lived there all my life. My grandfather built his home for the family shortly after arriving in Philadelphia from France. I was the third generation of my family to have lived there." She broke down in tears and hurried out of the dining room. Will followed, trying to console her. Annie was overwhelmed with pent-up emotions, feelings of loss she had suppressed until now. Her breakdown was made worse by doing so in front of her audience. She'd been taught to never show her true feelings to an audience.

Back in their room, Annie said, "It was embarrassing to have lost my composure during a performance."

Will assured Annie the audience were her friends.

They cared for her. No one had known the fire that killed so many had also destroyed her home. Will held Annie tightly in his arms until the angels of sleep carried her away.

A light knock was heard at the door. It was Mr. Bidermann inquiring about Annie. Will stepped out into the hallway to avoid waking her.

Mr. Bidermann asked, "How is she, Will?"

"Sleeping now." Will closed the door and they moved to a settee in an alcove of the hallway.

Mr. Bidermann said, "What can Evelina and I do? We had no idea Annie lived near our warehouse. Why didn't you say something when I took you there yesterday?"

Will said, "I didn't know what to say! So much happened at once." Will shook his head. "Life here is hectic. I'm bewildered by all the people! The streets paved in cobblestone, indoor plumbing, and now telegrams! I just want to go home, to sit on the porch and watch the sun set over the Rio Grande."

"That sounds good to me, Will, with what's going on around here."

They made plans to get Will upriver to Philadelphia by carriage. He would send the telegram to Governor Bell, then check out of the Girard House. Bidermann would send a wagon for their belongings.

Mr. Bidermann said, "Will, I know you must return to Texas. Evelina and I have discussed it. We will care for Annie at Winterthur for as long as she needs us. Then we will build and furnish her a home in Philadelphia or at Winterthur, whichever she prefers. Last night's dinner guests established a fund. DuPont matched all donations, raising thirty-one thousand dollars for victims of the fire. The City of Philadelphia has already appropriated ten thousand dollars in assistance for the victims."

"I know Annie will appreciate your generosity, Mr. Bidermann. I will tell her the good news when she awakes."

Mr. Bidermann rose. "Get a good night's sleep. You're going to need it. See you at daybreak!"

Will could not sleep, thinking of all the things he must do before leaving for Texas. The one he dreaded most was saying goodbye to Annie, who slept beside him. The coachman knocked on the door at six. Annie woke as Will was dressing.

Annie said, "What's going on? Why are you up so early?"

"I'm going to Philadelphia to send a telegraph."

Annie said, "That's crazy! Evelina told me last night that Mr. Bidermann has a telegraph machine in his office. Why go to Philadelphia?"

"It must be sent from Philadelphia!" Will hastily buttoned his shirt.

Annie said, "We will be in Philadelphia this afternoon! Why make two trips just for a telegram?"

"I'll explain when I return!" Will had no idea of how he was going to explain his secret mission to her.

"Will Smith, if you're trying to dump me—" Annie looked into Will's eyes for an answer.

"No, Annie, I wouldn't do that. If you feel like going, dress quickly and meet me in front. Leave your things here; we're coming back." Will went downstairs. Two teamsters waited on an empty wagon. The impatient coachman hurried Will and Annie into an open carriage, explaining that he was ordered to get Will to the telegraph station by the time it opened.

The sun was rising as Mr. Bidermann saw them off. The wagon would go to the Girard House for their things.

The carriage could take Will and Annie to the telegraph station, then deliver them to the hotel before the freight wagon arrived.

Will had much to explain to Annie. He started with the good news, that the Bidermanns would build her a new home and furnish it. She could stay at Winterthur if she wished, until her home was finished. The news that her neighbors were going to be provided for made Annie happy.

"What about us?" Annie looked at Will.

Will said, "Annie, I must get back to Texas. I'm on a leave of absence from my duties as sheriff."

"I know." Annie looked sadly up at Will. "I was hoping you would stay with me a while longer. I know Mr. Bidermann would give you a job at DuPont."

Will asked, "How would you know that?"

Annie answered, "I heard Mr. Bidermann say that last night. He also mentioned you were his agent for DuPont in Texas. He spoke well of you, Will."

Will said, "Annie, my friends and family are in Texas. You met my nephew Fayette. I would like to see him and my nieces grow up, and I miss my brothers and sister. Texas is my home!"

Annie said, "I know." She touched Will's face. They kissed passionately as they rode along in silence, the only sound the beat of horse hooves.

Will pondered an idea for a moment. Then he blurted it out without thinking it through. "Annie, my friend Clay Davis is building a beautiful hotel in Rio Grande City. It's going to have a huge stage and ballroom for entertainment. Come to Texas with me! You can perform there. I can make it happen."

Annie said, "Thank you, Will. I may go on a tour of Texas again." She looked away to hide her tears. "I could never live there." Shaking her head, she went on, "Indians stealing little children in broad daylight. Your father and brother brutally murdered by savages!"

Will said, "I thought you liked Texas."

Annie looked into Will's eyes. "Texas is an untamed land. I'm proud to have met those like you who are attempting to tame it, but I could never live there." Annie shook her head.

"I understand Annie. I'll miss you." Will held her in his arms, thinking, *What a foolish idea! Inviting Annie to come to Rio Grande City to work for my jealous girlfriend.*

The carriage arrived at the telegraph office just as station master James Donovan was unlocking the door.

Will told the carriage driver and Annie he would only be a few minutes.

James Donovan said, "Good morning, Mr....Smith. What a surprise, seeing you again so soon."

Will handed Donovan the form and said, "Mr. Donovan, I need you to send this telegram."

"Back to Texas, I assume?" Mr. Donovan looked at the form.

Will nodded. "The message is to Texas Governor Bell, in Austin. The contents must be confidential."

Mr. Donovan straightened up and said, "All Washington Telegraph Company messages are confidential, as they are sent in Morse Code. I can assure you it's confidential, Mr. Smith."

"Texas doesn't have telegraph services. How will this get to Austin, and when will it arrive?" Will glanced at the apparatus that would send the message.

"Your telegram will reach our office in New Orleans in a few minutes. Then it will be placed in a sealed envelope and given to the first packet ship leaving for Galveston. The first stage line leaving Galveston will take it to Austin."

"How long do you think that will take?" Will asked.

Mr. Donovan said, "After the wire reaches New Orleans, it's up to the weather and connections in Texas. It should be in Galveston in a couple of days, maybe three more by stage; figure on five to seven days."

Will watched as Mr. Donovan tapped the short message. Will paid and headed to the waiting carriage.

By noon, word had reached President Fillmore that Texas was preparing to invade New Mexico Territory. The Governor of Mississippi had already sent word to the president that should federal troops attempt to stop Texas from defending their boundaries, he would send troops to New Mexico to support Texas. If that happened, the president knew other slave states might join in the effort. President Fillmore did not need a civil war on his watch.

The Compromise of 1850 needed the boundary issue resolved. President Fillmore asked both houses of Congress to consider a counteroffer for the sixty-seven million acres of disputed land. Senator James Pearce of Maryland, a friend of Mr. Bidermann and other creditors, suggested paying Texas's debts. Only Sam Houston, Thomas Rusk, and a handful of creditors knew how destitute the State of Texas was. The Texas skullduggery had worked.

Will and Annie made it back to Winterthur by noon.

They said their rather painful goodbyes and Will boarded a well-marked DuPont keelboat loaded with sand and covered with oilcloth. Meanwhile, the munitions were placed on an armed clipper ship. It would rendezvous with the decoy keelboat at sundown near Cape May in the Bay of Delaware. Will would board the clipper ship loaded with the munitions and sail directly to Galveston.

Mr. Bidermann urged, "Will, you must get through the Port of Philadelphia before word of the shipment of munitions gets to the Revenue Cutter Service."

Will said, "I know. Thank you for everything."

Mr. Bidermann signaled the skipper to shove off.

"Take care of Annie!" Will waved.

Mr. Bidermann nodded. Will sat down on the forward stow box for the trip down the Delaware. As the boat rounded the first bend at Brandywine Creek, there stood Evelina and Annie waving. He stood and waved back, a lump in his throat and a tear in his eye, not knowing if he would ever see Annie again.

Chapter Twenty-Four

 ill knew once the munitions were in open waters of the Atlantic, flying the American flag, they would be safe.

While waiting for the clipper ship, Will used the last rays of daylight to pen letters to family and friends. He took pleasure knowing they would be impressed by receiving mail from so far away. The keelboat operator would take the letters back to Wilmington for mailing.

As the sun set, cumulus clouds blocked the light of a half moon. Will saw the silhouette of a ship dropping its sails, then the clammer of the anchor chain descending rapidly over the side.

"Is it our ship?" Will whispered to the keelboat captain, who was holding a rifle at the ready. The captain didn't answer but motioned for Will to be quiet. They both saw the light on the ship signal them.

The captain said, "I think this be who we wait for!" He laid down his gun and picked up a lantern and lit it.

The oars could be heard, stroking in cadence. A dinghy approached with two oarsmen. Once beside the keelboat, the crews of both vessels whispered in French. The captain nodded to Will and said, "All is good! Have a safe journey."

Will handed his baggage to the forward rower. When they

reached the clipper ship, Will chose to climb the ropes instead of riding in the bosun's chair.

The clipper ship was named *Evelina* for Bidermann's wife. The one-hundred-twenty-foot ship had a crew of twelve. With three masts and favorable winds, it could make it to Texas in ten days.

Will was assigned the portside stateroom. Reading from the ship's log found on the small desk, he learned this was the personal ship of the Bidermann family. The elegant stateroom had a large collection of leather-bound books. Unfortunately, they were written in French. The crew spoke only French. The captain spoke a little English, but not enough to carry on a worthwhile conversation. Will wiled away the time whittling on a small block of wood found on the foredeck. He watched the swells of the ocean and an occasional seabird overhead. With time to ponder, his thoughts turned to the women in his life.

Will's feelings for Norma were different from those for Annie. He assumed talk and suspicions of Norma killing Frenchy Berlandier may have compromised his intimacy toward her. He wrote a long letter to Annie, to be delivered by the captain along with Will's carving of a dove.

The *Evelina* docked in Galveston on the tenth day out of Philadelphia. Texas Rangers under the command of Captain John Ford waited on the wharf for the munitions to arrive. Their orders were to deliver them to Austin. A two-hundred-yard tunnel, dug from the Capitol to the General Land Office would house the arsenal. The tunnel had been dug to protect state employees from Indian raids and would now be used to hide munitions paid for by the Federal Government.

Chapter Twenty-Five

*O*nce the Rangers took possession of the munitions, Will's mission was accomplished. He would stay at the Tremont House on the Galveston Strand. On the way to the hotel, he stopped at the Star Drug Store and purchased a New Orleans *Picayune* newspaper, cigars, and a bottle of whiskey.

Biding time on the upstairs porch of the Tremont for three days, Will read the *Picayune*. He learned his friend, George W. Kendall, had sold his interest in the *Picayune* newspaper and bought a sheep ranch northwest of San Antonio. The story mentioned that the two-volume memoir Kendall wrote, *Narrative of the Texas Santa Fe Expedition*, was selling well. Will was proud of his old friend, who had accomplished many of his goals in life.

A story about Dr. Jean Louis Berlandier caught Will's attention. *Could this Dr. Berlandier be Frenchy?* Will remembered Frenchy saying he was the only Berlandier in the Americas. The article said the doctor was the administrator of the hospital in Matamoras, Mexico, across the Rio Grande from Brownsville. Will tore the article from the paper, folded it neatly, and then stuffed it in his vest pocket.

Smoke bellowing from the stacks of the steamboat *Corvette* announced its arrival long before it appeared on the horizon. This trip, Captain Kenedy would be at the helm. The crew would unload its cargo on arrival then load up in the morning, leaving at noon to arrive in Brownsville two days later.

The next day, Captain Kenedy was waiting at the end of the gangway. He welcomed Will with open arms. "We thought you were dead! No one knew where you were. I asked Clay Davis often about you."

Will smiled and said, "It will be good to be home."

"Where have you been?" Captain Kenedy waited for an answer which didn't come.

Will asked, "Is the *Corvette* going all the way to Rio Grande City?"

Captain Kenedy replied, "Yes, with stops in Matagorda, Corpus, and Brownsville."

"Would I have time to go to the hospital in Matamoras, across the river from Brownsville, while you load supplies for Fort Ringgold?"

Captain Kenedy looked surprised. "Are you ill?"

"No, Captain, I'm investigating an old case. Someone who works there might have answers to help close it."

"Don't you worry; take my horse and carriage. We'll wait for you."

"That's quite generous, Captain." Will reached for his wallet.

Captain Kenedy shook his head. "You know I don't charge men of the law."

A crewmember escorted Will to a communal stateroom below decks. It had two sets of double bunks side by side. Will placed his belongings under a bottom bunk, then peeked out the small porthole to see that the boat was slowly moving away from the dock. He went topside for a better view. Will had become a seasoned seafarer and knew what made a steamship move. He saw both crewmen frantically stoking wood into the burners. He lent a hand, passing firewood as Captain Kenedy pushed the throttle to the max.

Will, sensing the crew's urgency, asked, "What's the big hurry?"

"A blue norther is blowing in." The lead crewman pointed north.

Dark blue clouds blotted out the sun in that direction. Only darkness lay behind the clouds as the storm engulfed them. The temperature dropped. Swells bounced the *Corvette* fore and aft. Captain Kenedy fought the ship's wheel, keeping it on its southernly course. The next port was Matagorda, fifteen hours away. It was a rough night on the water. Fortunately, the storm blew through as fast as it had arrived, like most Texas northers.

The sun was up when three dolphins greeted the *Corvette* entering Matagorda Bay. Will watched the dolphins intently as they guided Captain Kenedy to the wharf at Indianola. Will had heard about the friendly dolphins in Matagorda Bay. He was impressed with his first sighting of the chattering creatures.

While the crew unloaded and loaded, Will took a walk around the thriving hamlet of Indianola, previously known as Indian Point.

When he heard the whistle of the *Corvette* blowing, he knew it was time for him to reboard.

Captain Kenedy asked, "What do you think of Indianola?"

Will said, "It appears to have more homes than Austin."

Captain Kenedy said, "I'm told Indianola has twice as many people."

At Corpus Christi, Captain Kenedy, anxious to be home, was relieved by his partner, Captain Richard King. The La Parra Ranch south of Corpus Christi was the home of Mifflin and Petra Kenedy. King and Kenedy continued to purchase Spanish land grants, eventually becoming the largest landholders in South Texas.

Mifflin informed King that Will needed a carriage to cross the border to Matamoros, Mexico. King sent an armed guard to stay with the carriage while Will took care of business.

Walking into the Matamoros hospital, Will saw the man he knew as Frenchy talking to an attractive nurse. Their conversation was short. It was obvious they were more than business associates.

"May I help you?" The man asked.

Will said, "Frenchy, it's me, Will Smith, the Texas Ranger—"

"Yes, Will! I remember you. We met in Piedras Negras many years ago." He looked around to see who might be listening. "Come, let's go to my office."

The administrator's office was only steps away. Will followed him into a well-lit room with many windows. Plants were growing everywhere. Will remembered reading Frenchy's notes and seeing his drawings of his plants. A small sign on the desk read "Dr. Jean Louis Berlandier, Oficina de la Administradar."

"It's good to see you again, Will! Did you make it to

California to marry the girl?"

Will reached into his vest pocket and pulled out the small gold ring to show Frenchy.

Frenchy said, "It was the winter of forty-two we met. You still have the ring?"

"Yes, I still carry it." Will put the ring back in his pocket.

"Obviously you didn't find the girl." Frenchy leaned back in his chair.

Will told Frenchy the sad story of his trip to California, in the dead of winter eight years ago. Frenchy listened quietly as Will told the story of finding Bella, married with a child, and expecting another. He didn't mention the oldest was his.

Frenchy looked sad after hearing Will's story. "I'm sorry, Will, that it didn't work out for you." Frenchy leaned forward and changed the subject. "What brings you here to Matamoros Hospital?"

Will said, "I read in the New Orleans *Picayune* that a Dr. Jean Louis Berlandier was running the hospital. I thought it might be you!"

"I'm honored that you would do that." Frenchy stood and extended his right hand, giving Will a hearty handshake and said, "Taking the time out of your busy schedule, to come across the border to find me."

Will said, "I was on my way to Davis Landing. I had to know, Frenchy, if you were the Berlandier in the paper. I'm glad to know you are alive and well. My carriage is waiting, and I must get back to the boat."

"Thank you, Will. I'm honored you searched me out. Please, come again when you have more time."

On the ride back to the *Corvette,* Will felt remorse that he had ever suspected Norma of killing Frenchy and burying him near her cantina in Piedras Negras. He also felt relieved that he now knew the truth.

Captain King was blowing the whistle of the *Corvette* as Will's carriage neared the wharf. The driver shook the reins and the horse moved into a trot.

Both burners were red hot and the crew held the lines to cast off when Will jumped on.

Captain King bellowed, "Just in time!"

Will nodded and sat on a keg of beer that was headed to the troops at Fort Ringgold. He lit his last cigar as the steamboat chugged out of Brownsville.

Chapter Twenty-Six

Things always looked the same on the river with two names. A shack here and there, usually miles apart. On either side of the river the *casitas* always had a donkey, chickens, dogs, and lots of goats. Captain King enjoyed blowing the horn near the casitas. The children and parents always ran out to wave. The children made the familiar sign to blow the horn. The donkeys brayed, dogs barked, and children screamed with delight when Captain King pulled the cord of the steam engine, releasing just enough steam to engage the horn.

Will had left Davis Landing at Rio Grande City on a hot August day and was returning forty-one days later. Captain King postponed the sad news he had for Will until near the end of the trip.

Once the boat was tied up and the engines shut down, Will began gathering his things, anxious to see Norma again.

Captain King said, "Please sit down, Will. I need to tell you something."

Will sat down, knowing that when Captain King spoke, he had something important to say.

Captain King said, "My friend and business partner, Captain Kenedy, could not find the words to tell you. So, he left me with this difficult task to bear."

Will leaned back on the rails of the *Corvette*, his arms crossed at the waist, looking at his worn boots. Waiting to hear the news Mifflin Kenedy couldn't tell him, Will thought, *It must be bad.*

Captain King finally said, "Norma is dead. She died in her sleep."

Will was stunned. "No! That can't be."

"I'm sorry, Will." Captain King shook his head.

"What happened?" Will asked.

"Cholera took her two weeks ago. Several of her girls had it, but she was the only one to die. Major LaMotte sent medics from Fort Ringgold. They did everything they could to save her."

Will looked forlornly at Captain King and shook his head. "I had just decided to ask her to marry me."

Captain King continued, "No one knew where you went after leaving Austin. Clay Davis sent word to your family in Austin. Captain Kenedy and I carried Clay's letter to Galveston, where I placed it on the stage to Austin, addressed to your brother Fenwick at the stage line office."

"Where did they...bury Norma?" Will asked with a gulp.

Captain King said, "In that part of the cemetery reserved for victims of cholera."

Will asked, "Did she suffer?"

Captain King said, "I don't know, Will. All I know is, having survived cholera as a child, it wasn't an easy death."

Will nodded, his lips tightened as he picked up his gear. "Thank you, Captain King, for the ride and letting me know about Norma." He started to turn away.

Captain King put his hand on Will's shoulder and said, "There is something else you must know."

"What is it?" Will stood, clenching his bags.

Captain King said, "The Starr County Board appointed a new sheriff last week."

"I see!" Will said, biting his lip to keep his emotions under control.

Captain King continued, "Mifflin and I have been talking about it. If you want a job, you can work for us! We will pay you better than Starr County pays its sheriff."

Will said, "Thanks for the offer. Let me sleep on it a week or two. Let's talk on your next run."

Will walked slowly up the incline toward the center of town. He gazed at the partially completed hotel Clay Davis was building for Norma's Cantina. When he reached the Rio Hotel, he found Alejandra serving dinner to customers.

Alejandra said, "Thank goodness you are alive!" She hugged Will, "I told everyone you would be back. You sit, I will fix you your favorite meal—carne asada!"

"That would be great." Will set down his bags and took a seat at his usual table.

After his first warm meal in days, Will was ready for bed. Alejandra had kept his room just as it was and dusted it every week. Will climbed the stairs to his room overlooking the square. He felt at home, even if he was no longer the sheriff.

Waking to the sound of a rooster crowing, Will was stiff and sore from the long journey and twelve hours in his feather bed. He moved around his room slowly and tried not to wake anyone else in the hotel. Alejandra's knock let him know coffee was at his door. He wondered how she knew when he was awake. He made good use of the pitcher of water and wash bowl, shaving off a two-week-old beard and trimming his thick moustache. Will was ready to go to work, but for the first time in years, he did not have a job to go to.

Will took a walk around the town. Little had changed other than the new hotel being built. He walked by the gate at the entrance to Fort Ringgold. Will didn't recognize the duty guard but said hello and waved at him. His walk led to the city cemetery that Clay and Hilaria Davis had set aside for the town's dead. He found Norma's freshly dug grave on the last row away from town. Wilted flowers left by her many friends covered the mound. Will told Norma he found Frenchy in Matamoros and he intended to tell everyone that she did not murder him. Will thought, *It's ironic that I solved a crime that never happened and the accused is now dead.* He pulled the gold ring out of his pocket and pushed it into the fresh soil next to her wooden cross.

Back at the Rio, Will had his usual large breakfast of eggs and bacon with several tortillas. He heard a commotion. It was Clay Davis in the foyer being greeted by Alejandra and her two teenage girls, Leticia and Sophia.

Once Clay had exchanged pleasantries and presented gifts to his sister-in-law and nieces, he came into the dining room to welcome Will home and to offer his condolences.

Clay said, "I'm sorry Will, about Norma. She had good care to the end. There was nothing anyone could do."

Will nodded, his mouth full of food.

Clay pulled out a chair and sat down. "I'm glad you're home. We didn't know what happened to you after you resigned and left for Austin for who knows where."

Will raised his eyebrows. "I didn't resign! I asked you for a temporary leave of absence in my letter to you in August, and you knew damn well where I went."

Clay tilted his head and said, "I assume you know the county board voted to replace you?"

Will turned in his chair. "Yes, Captain King told me, at the landing."

Clay said, "Richard King, Mifflin Kenedy, and Major La-Motte were quite upset at the board removing you and putting someone in with no experience."

Will asked, "Who did they appoint?"

Clay said, "Domingo de la Garza."

Will sputtered and said, "They chose your eighteen-year-old nephew...to be sheriff of a county larger than the State of Tennessee? What the hell were they thinking, Clay? They are going to get Domingo killed!"

Clay Davis raised his bushy eyebrows. "It seems Domingo was the only person that wanted the job. I'm sorry, Will! The board made their decision. As you know, the statutes say any county official that abandons his post for more than thirty-one days may be replaced by a majority vote of the board. That's what they did!"

Will said, "Thirty-one days?"

Clay added, "That's what the statues say."

"How in the hell did you let that happen?" Will pushed his plate away.

Clay said, "I'm the state senator now, no longer the county judge. I have no seat on the county board. I had nothing to do with your being replaced as sheriff. My wife and her family are all flustered at me like I could have overridden the board's decision. I've spent the last two weeks bearing gifts, trying to dig myself out of the shit hole I'm in. I don't want Domingo hurt either! He is like a son to me."

Will said, "Clay, they can't replace me. What they have done is illegal."

Clay asked, "Why do you say it is illegal?"

Will said, "You just said the board may replace any county official that has abandoned their post for more than thirty-one days. I got here last night. My request for a temporary leave of absence was dated August twenty-first. Count the days. I arrived ready to go to work yesterday! If my math is correct, yesterday was thirty days."

Clay said, "But we left Rio Grande City for Austin on the tenth of August." Clay pulled out his journal to be sure.

Will said, "I left Starr County with you! At your request, on the tenth! You asked me to go after getting the board's approval, for protection of you and Clements. My request for a leave of absence was dated the twenty-first of August, while still with you in Austin. I was in Austin on Starr County business, same as you and Clements until August twenty-first."

Clay stared at Will while his mind did the math in his head. "You're right, Will. The new county judge asked me when we left Starr County. You were still on county business until the twenty-first. After that you were on a mission for the State of Texas. Which, by the way, Governor Bell described as a damn good job!"

Will said, "Then you agree with me."

"Yes, Will. It was my mistake! I'll notify the county judge immediately. You did not abandon your post beyond thirty-one days. I'll be back to you after I speak with the judge." Clay stood and placed a reassuring hand on Will's shoulder. "I've got your back on this."

Will said, "Thank you."

After Clay left, Alejandra came with more coffee. Will asked her to sit with him. She sat down and reached across the table for his hands. Alejandra peered into his blue eyes. Will leaned toward her.

"I'm sorry, Will. I want you to know that Norma loved you! She told me so many times. How you make her happy. I lose two good men and I loved them both."

Will smiled, which he seldom did.

Alejandra said, "That didn't sound right." She shook her head, "You know what I mean. I didn't love them both at the same time."

Will said, "I understand what you meant. I didn't know your husband, but I know W.G. loved you."

Alejandra said, "Then why did W.G. leave me and go to California?"

Will said, "He wanted you to go with him. He told me he asked you, and you said no."

Alejandra said, "Yes, I say no to him then! Now that my Leticia is getting married, Sophia and I will be alone. Now I think I make a mistake by not marrying W.G. and going to California with him."

Will said, "Sometimes, circumstances in our lives like time, place, and family, make for difficult decisions that we must live with."

Alejandra asked, "Why didn't you marry Norma?"

Will leaned back in his chair and said, "She never asked me."

Alejandra said, "The man should ask the woman, Will!" They both grinned.

Alejandra got up to wait on two soldiers that came in from Fort Ringgold.

The front porch of the Rio beckoned Will to his rickety old chair. The high back chair from the dining room stood in the same spot where Will had left it. He missed the old chair and its view of Main Street. Every morning after breakfast, Will had sat and whittled as he watched who came and went. If he was needed, the locals knew where to find him.

Clay Davis came with good news and a plan that would be agreeable to all. Will would complete his term as Sheriff of Starr County. He would be on the ballot as the incumbent in the November election. Domingo de la Garza had filed to run for sheriff, but would be Will's deputy for now.

Will said, "That's good. I'll have eight weeks to train Domingo. Have you told him I'm back?"

Clay Davis said, "Yes, and Domingo is excited to hear you are home. He has been living with Hilaria and me since his appointment. Domingo is at the newspaper office helping the new editor get today's edition out."

What Clay didn't tell Will was that the front page of the paper had originally announced the appointment of the new sheriff. A new edition was being printed that read Will was home and Domingo was his new deputy.

Clay said, "Domingo will be over as soon as the paper is finished. Everyone is glad you're home." Clay patted Will on the back. "Will, protect Domingo and teach him well. I doubt he has ever been in a fistfight, much less a gunfight."

Will said, "I'll do my best." Clay walked across the dusty street to his home.

Will entered the dining room to be greeted by the daughters of Alejandra. Their mother was busy preparing for the quinceañera of Sophia and the wedding of Leticia.

Will asked, "Quinceañera? So Sophia is going to be fifteen years old?"

Alejandra said, "Yes, she already is, and Leticia is now seventeen years old." Alejandra picked up the wedding dress to continue stitching the sides.

Will nodded and asked, "Where is my mail?"

Alejandra said, "Where I always put your papers! On your table in the dining room." She watched Will as he sorted through a month's worth of mail.

Will sat in one of the two chairs at a table for six in the Rio's dining room. The table was the official Starr County sheriff's office, now covered with mail, newspapers, and wanted posters. Alejandra kept all the paperwork in neat little stacks, secured by the weight of smooth rocks from the river. Will read the wanted posters received from other jurisdictions. Rio Grande City was a fugitive gateway to Mexico for bandits running from the law. Will hung the posters in the hotel lobby. Extra copies were taken to the ferry operators. They could earn a year's pay helping with the capture of one bandit.

Two letters postmarked from California caught Will's immediate attention. One was marked Los Angeles, the other San Francisco. The San Francisco letter was from the sheriff's department and the other was from his friend W.G. Dryden. Will thought, *Why would the sheriff of San Francisco be writing him?*

To Will's surprise, the letter was from his longtime friend and captain during his days as a Texas Ranger. John "Jack" Coffee Hays was now the first Sheriff of San Francisco County. Hay's letter told of all the exciting things happening in California since gold had been discovered at Sutter's Mill two years before. Hays invited Will to come to San Francisco to be his chief deputy. He wrote, "I will pay you double whatever Starr County is paying. I need a man I can trust. Good men are hard to find in these parts. San Francisco has become a haven for prostitutes, gamblers, and all kinds of hustlers. Please answer posthaste as I need to fill the chief deputy position by the end of the year."

Will opened the letter from Los Angeles, which was from W.G. Dryden, advising him of how wonderful things were in Southern California. W.G. had been appointed Los Angeles City Clerk and was acting as city attorney, helping the mayor and aldermen organize the municipality of Los Angeles. He offered Will the job of city marshal, if he wanted it.

Will was overwhelmed and confused, yet excited about receiving two job offers in one day. His mind was spinning, thinking about going to California, yet he was sad, thinking about leaving his friends and family in Texas.

Alejandra came to Will's table. She sat down across from him with that look he knew so well, her hands in her lap, her shoulders straight, gazing at him.

Will asked, "Alejandra, do you need something?"

Alejandra said, "Yes. I see you read your letter from W.G." She sighed. "I receive my letter from him, the same day your letter come." Alejandra twiddled her thumbs impatiently, waiting for Will to tell her what W.G. had to say.

Will laid down the letter from W.G. and leaned toward her. "W.G. wants me to go to Los Angeles. He wants me to be the city marshal."

Alejandra said, "Will you go to California?"

Will saw Domingo coming in. "I don't know, Alejandra! I must think about it."

"Me, too!" Alejandra saw Domingo coming. "Please tell nobody about this."

"We can talk later." Will turned his attention to Domingo.

Domingo wore a shiny new badge, carved from a silver dollar. Strapped to his waist was a rusty-looking pistol that was a remnant of the War of 1812.

Will said, "You look ready to be a lawman. Where did you get the gun?"

"It was my father's during the Mexican American War."

"Can I see it?" Will motioned for the gun and Domingo handed it over.

Will examined the single shot pistol and handed it back to Domingo. "No wonder Mexico lost the war!"

Domingo said, chagrined, "When the Americans start the war, old guns were all Mexico had."

Will said, "Mexico was outgunned. Let that be a lesson! Never be outgunned! That's rule number one! Rule number two: make every shot count! Today we're going to the shooting range at Fort Ringgold to practice."

Domingo boyishly smiled, revealing his perfect shiny white teeth. Will thought, *Domingo looks more like a priest than a lawman.*

They walked the short distance to Fort Ringgold to see Major LaMotte, commander of the fort. Will and Domingo reminisced along the way about their first meeting with Major LaMotte. They laughed about the events of that day two years before.

At headquarters, they were greeted by Commander LaMotte's aide-de-camp. "Major LaMotte has someone in his office now. He is quite busy today! Is he expecting you?"

Will said, "I'm sure he isn't, but we'll see him anyhow!"

The aide didn't understand or appreciate Will's snide remark. "I'll tell him you are waiting."

They heard Major LaMotte say, "Send them in! I always

have time to see the local sheriff."

Will said, "Thanks, Major. I came to personally introduce you to my new deputy, Domingo de la Garza, whom you already know."

Major LaMotte said, "Congratulations to you both! I've been saying Starr County needed more law enforcement since the day I arrived. Domingo is a good choice, as he knows everyone in the county and is kin to most."

Will nodded his head in agreement. He and Major La-Motte both knew Domingo's biggest obstacle would be his many friends and family, who might take advantage of their relationship.

Will said, "Domingo and I are here to ask permission to use your firing range for his training."

Major LaMotte said, "I can do better than that. I can put Domingo through six weeks of basic training here at Fort Ringgold." Major LaMotte glanced at Domingo's gun. "Is that the service gun you're planning to use?"

"Yes, sir," Domingo looked down at the floor, obviously embarrassed. "It's all I have."

Major LaMotte said, "I have the guns you need!" He opened his safe and pulled out two Colt Walker revolvers. "These are compliments of the U.S. Army and Samuel Colt."

Domingo said in surprise, "They're just like Will's! Thank you, Major LaMotte!" and admired the shiny new guns' appearance.

Major LaMotte said, "They are single action revolvers with six rounds each. Your fire power has been increased dramatically." Major LaMotte pulled out two boxes of cartridges. "These will get you started on the firing range."

Domingo smiled, "Thank you again, Major LaMotte."

"You're welcome." Major LaMotte stepped to the door and

asked his aide to take Domingo to the quartermaster's office to complete the guns' transfer from the Army to the Starr County Sheriff's office.

Once Domingo and the aide left the office, Major LaMotte returned to his desk and sat down. "Will, what the hell were you thinking, hiring Domingo? He's still wet behind the ears!"

"I didn't hire him. The county board hired Domingo to be sheriff in my absence, without my knowledge or consent. They assumed I wasn't coming back. Clay said he was the only applicant for the job. The family is deeply concerned for Domingo's safety. I can't go anywhere until Domingo is ready."

Major LaMotte said, "When Domingo was the officers' stable boy, he was a hard worker, fast learner, and appreciated constructive criticism. Everyone liked him. I believe Domingo could make a good soldier or lawman…in a few years."

Will said, "All I have is a few weeks!" Will shifted in his chair and leaned toward LaMotte. "Major, I need to keep this quiet until after the election. I've been offered the job as the city marshal in Los Angeles. That's why Domingo's training is so important. I can't leave Starr County without a competent replacement."

Major LaMotte asked, "How in the world did you get a job offer from California?"

Will explained, "From the man who recommended me for this job as Starr County sheriff. Jack Hays, now the Sheriff of San Francisco County. I also got an offer from W.G. to be the City Marshal of Los Angeles. I'm taking W.G.'s offer. They want me there by the first of the year."

Major La Motte said, "Congratulations, Will! You'll make a good marshal for Los Angeles. We're starting some training for a small group of new recruits next week. Domingo could be taught the basics of combat, teamwork, and discipline.

You will have to teach him about the law."

Will said, "I like that idea. Let's ask Domingo when he returns."

Domingo liked the idea and asked to stay with the soldiers in the barracks. It was agreed he would live, train, and bivouac as a soldier of the U.S. Army. His fellow soldiers would assume he was a soldier just like them.

At the firing range, Will taught Domingo to break down the Colt Walkers, then put them back together again. Domingo practiced handling the guns as Will watched him draw, aim, and fire. Once Domingo was comfortable with the revolvers, Will gave him six cartridges to load and unload.

Will watched Domingo intently load the shells, which he did with ease after a few tries. Will thought, *That's good, but could he reload with someone shooting at him?*

"Tell me Domingo, why did you apply for the job of sheriff?"

Domingo said, "From the moment I first see you ride into town, I want to be like you. A man of the law protecting the citizens of the Nueces Strip. I watch you concerned for the people and the soldiers during the epidemic. That is why I volunteer for your job when you don't come back. We had no one to fill your boots. I'm glad you come back to teach me how to be a lawman."

Will had never received a compliment like that from anyone. He grasped for the right response to his protégé.

Will said, "Thank you, Domingo. I hope I can live up to your expectations, as you and I are a team now! We must anticipate every move the other one makes. Like a team of horses working side by side pulling a wagon. Do you understand how important that is?"

"Yes, I understand. I will do my best to learn from you!" Domingo broke into his trademark smile, displaying a mouth full of teeth. "I will do whatever you say."

Will said, "I want you to grow a moustache, and try not to smile so much."

Domingo asked, "Why? My mother always say smile at people you meet."

Will said, "Domingo, that's good at church or with family and friends. You're not an altar boy anymore! You're a deputy sheriff now. There will be run-ins with people that want to kill you because you are the law. Never forget that! You must look and talk tough. Your smile might win over a beautiful girl, but it could get your ass killed. Do you understand?"

Domingo said, "Yes, sir!"

Will said, "Let's do some shooting." Domingo flashed his trademark smile again. Will unholstered both guns and shot several rounds toward Domingo's fast-moving feet.

Domingo shouted, "Why you shoot at my feet?"

Will said, "To make a point! From now on when you smile that big friendly smile, I'm going to start shooting until that smile goes away."

Domingo frowned at Will, who said, "There you go! Now you're getting it. Keep that frown on your face when you're wearing the badge."

Domingo asked, "Why you want me to grow a moustache?"

Will explained, "It may help cover some of that smile and make you appear older than you are."

Domingo said, "The people here know me as their altar boy. They wouldn't hurt me."

Will said, "When I was about your age, the closest I ever came to being killed was by a pretty girl. She looked so sweet and innocent but had just swindled a bank. I turned my back for a moment, and this is what she did!" Will pulled his shirt off his shoulder. Domingo grimaced at seeing the nasty scar there.

Will told Alejandra he was taking W.G.'s offer of City Marshal of Los Angeles. If she wanted to go, she could travel with him. He was leaving Rio Grande City on the first of December by stage to Mazatlán, Mexico, arriving around mid-December. From Mazatlán, they would sail to the Port of Los Angeles.

Alejandra appreciated the offer. She had been praying about going to California. She said, "Will, this is my home where my girls were born. All my family and friends live here. As much as I love W.G., I cannot go with you to California. I belong here in Rio Grande City."

Chapter Twenty-Seven

The rigorous training at Fort Ringgold burned off the puffiness of his Aunt Hilarias's tacos. Domingo looked fit and ready to fight. He earned the marksmanship medal and a promotion to Private First Class, even though he was not in the Army. Afterward, his battle buddies were told Domingo was not a recruit but training to be Deputy Sheriff of Starr County. They razzed him about the deceit but praised him for going through forty-five days of hell with them.

Clay and Domingo arrived at the Rio Hotel in the Davis family carriage. Will said goodbye to Alejandra and her girls, who cried because Will was going to California. Living and working under the same roof for two years, they considered Will family. He had captured the man that tried to assault the girls. Will had escorted more than one vaquero out of the Rio who'd made improper advances toward Alejandra or her girls.

Alejandra and the girls were up before dawn preparing food for Will's two-day journey to Monterrey, Mexico. Alejandra said, "Will, if I were younger, we would go with you with no fear under your protection." Tears ran down her cheek. "Please give this to W.G.!" She gave Will an envelope, he put it in the food basket she had prepared. Alejandra and the girls hugged Will. Domingo shook Will's hand, but turned quickly away, not wanting Will to see his tears.

Will grinned and said, "Domingo, show me that frown or I'll start shooting!"

Domingo said, "Thank you, Señor Will, for all you do for me."

Will put his hands on Domingo's shoulders and said, "You're a good man, Domingo. You will make Starr County a fine sheriff."

Domingo gave Will his best frown as he pulled his bags from the carriage. He was moving out on his own for the first-time, taking Will's room upstairs. His office would be the same corner table in the dining room of the Rio. Since Will had had no opponent in the Starr County election, the county board appointed Domingo sheriff for the duration of Will's term of office.

Clay and Will arrived at the stables in Camargo where a stagecoach driver and helper were harnessing a mud wagon to six sturdy mules. The driver Carlos and his helper Pedro recognized Clay and Will, as they had frequented Norma's Cantina. Both had been vaqueros on the de la Garza ranch before Señorita Hilaria Davis's father died. When her husband Clay took over his father-in-law's large ranching empire, many of the vaqueros chose not to work for the gringo. They moved to the Mexican side of the river. Now Carlos and Pedro had much respect for the good things Clay Davis had done for the Nueces Strip and the border town of Camargo.

Carlos said, "Buenos días, Señor Davis! What can we do for

you and the sheriff this morning?"

With a friendly smile, Clay replied, "Buenos días, Carlos! Your English has certainly improved since you told me to have sex with myself and left the rancho."

Carlos looked down at the ground, "I am sorry, Señor Davis. I should not say those things." He shook his head and looked at Clay. "I was not angry at you. I was angry the Americans moved the border and not tell me!" Pointing toward the river. "If I choose to live on the Nueces Strip, I no longer a Mexican!" Pedro nodded in agreement.

Clay said, "You two weren't the only people on the strip to be mad at me." Clay tied the reins and climbed down from the carriage. "Many Tejanos on the American side still feel that way."

Will handed down three bags to Pedro. One held his guns and ammo with two sets of handcuffs and shackles. Pedro complained to Carlos in Spanish that one bag was over twenty-five pounds. The baggage limit per person was twenty-five pounds.

Carlos asked, "Will, what is in the bag? It rattles like chains and is so heavy."

Will said, "Tools of my trade!"

"Guns and ammunition?" Carlos leaned over and whispered in Will's ear.

Will hesitated for a moment but nodded.

Carlos said, "Tools for mining! You will need those kinds of tools in California."

Will said, "How do you know I'm going to Calif—"

Carlos said, "Where else? Everyone is going to California these days to seek their fortune!" Carlos pointed toward the nearby bakery and café. "Those men from San Antonio are also going overland to Mazatlán."

Will said, "Carlos, I would greatly appreciate you not saying anything about who I am or what I do. Don't even let on that you know me, *por favor?*"

Carlos said, "Si, Señor Will." Then Carlos went about his business of harnessing the mules.

Clay handed a food basket to Will, "My wife baked a Johnny Cake for you. With what Alejandra cooked, you could feed everyone on your journey."

Will said, "Thank Hilaria for me, if you would." Will's hands were full. He nodded toward his fellow passengers. "Clay, take a good look at these two fellas coming toward us. When you get back to town, look at the wanted posters on my desk and in the lobby of the Rio. I recall seeing a flyer from somewhere on these hombres with a large reward for their capture."

Clay asked with concern, "If they are wanted, what can Domingo or I do about it?"

Will said, "Just remember who they are, in case something happens to me." Will climbed in through the small passenger door. Clay handed Will the basket full of food and said, "Have a safe trip."

Will said, "I'll write, soon as I get to Monterrey."

Clay nodded to Will that he understood, then turned to face the men. Clay looked them over and said good morning. The tall, slim one wore an eyepatch and had a moustache. His partner was short, clean shaven, and chubby, and only had his lower teeth; the top teeth were missing. Both men were overdressed for a long overland trip across northern Mexico. Will recognized the bulge of their waist coats and realized they were well armed.

Will instinctively felt for the small derringer in his boot. It gave him comfort knowing his backup gun was there.

The rear seat lifted up for storage. Will chose that seat facing forward after placing his bags under it. The wagon was different from those in the states. It accommodated four passengers if they sat closely, two facing forward and two facing back. The crude but sturdy wooden cab was built with two layers of ship-lap siding. It made the wagon heavier, but bulletproof inside the passenger compartment. The heavy wagon needed the six mules to pull it over the Sierra Madre Mountains.

Carlos popped the whip and whistled, the mules responded, and the wagon lurched forward. Once out of Camargo, Carlos slowed the mules to a steady trot.

Will pulled his hat down over his face and shut his eyes, pretending to fall asleep. He listened intently, as his fellow travelers seemed anxious about his presence. They whispered in what sounded like an Irish brogue and made wild hand gestures. Will watched them through a small hole in his hat.

Carlos stopped the mud wagon at the twenty-mile marker to water the mules in a running creek. Will pretended to sleep and waited for the strangers to exit. He raised his seat to retrieve his revolvers, which he buckled on. Once on the ground and out of the wagon, Will stretched before walking into the brush where he heard one of the men say, "What if he is—"

"Hush" the other one said, having heard Will's movement in the brush.

They were unusually afraid of him, and Will was determined to find out why. After finishing his business in the brush, Will looked for his travel companions, finding them standing under some shrub brush, chatting.

Will said, "I didn't catch your names back in Camargo. My name is Will Smith. What's yours?" Sticking out his hand to the tall man with a patch over his eye. They shook hands.

"Sean O'Reilly is my name. From...San Antonio," the tall one stammered.

The portly man mumbled, "My name is Robert Watts." He looked anxiously at the other man, as if he'd said something wrong. "We be half-brothers from the same mother, different fathers." He shook Will's hand. "That's why our last names... be different."

The half-brothers looked nothing alike. Their hands were rough like men who had done manual labor. The short one was nervous, while the tall one appeared cool and calculating. They claimed to be Irish immigrants, escaping the potato famine. The brothers said they learned the trade of a tailor in Ireland.

Will recognized their ill-fitting suits were of fine quality fabric like the ones the Busch Brothers had made for him in Saint Louis in 1841. He knew they were lying; no tailor would wear fine clothes that didn't fit. Robert, the short one, wore pants that were too long. Sean, the tall one, wore his too short. The clothes they had on were apparently tailored for the same man.

They headed back to the mud wagon. Even though it was December, it was a warm afternoon. The Irish brothers took their coats off and laid them on their seats.

Will said, "I've got plenty of food for everyone. Y'all sit down while I get it." He climbed into the cab for the food basket and a chance to see the tailor's label on the coats. Both suitcoats had the same label which read "This suit made for Robert B. Johnson, Galveston, Texas." *Who is this Robert Johnson?* Will wondered.

Will climbed down with the food basket in hand. He opened the basket on a long timber that had once been a mighty oak. The food was spread out for all to eat. Will and the so-called brothers, Robert and Sean, sat on another log. Pedro sat on a large boulder as Carlos stood to eat. No one said a word as they ate.

Will packed the remainder of the food back in the basket, then placed it in the cab, giving him an opportunity to look at the men's coats again. Will noticed their small leather carry-on had the initials R.B.J., the initials for Robert B. Johnson.

Will said, "Carlos, I need something out of my bag in the boot of the wagon."

Carlos said, "It's open."

Will pulled the tarp cover back to see the expensive leather luggage had the same initials. Now he was convinced these men were not who they said they were. Trying to remember where he had read about two men matching their descriptions, Will went back to the log, as Carlos wanted to talk to everyone. Pedro had finished harnessing the team and they were ready to roll.

Carlos said, "There is a small village, they call it China, in the State of Nuevo Leon." Carlos drew a line in the sand with a broken tree limb, "China is half the way between Camargo and Monterrey." He boldly marked the spot with an X.

"Why do they call it China?" asked Robert.

Carlos said, "I never know why they call it that."

Pedro said, "No Chinamen, just Mexicans in China." He laughed alone at his attempt at humor.

Carlos said, "I don't tell this when I have women passengers, it scares them too much! They beg me to take them back to Camargo."

Pedro said, "It is true, what Carlos say!" looking for approval from Carlos that did not come.

Carlos said, "I must tell you, the next sixty kilometers is the most dangerous portion of our trip. The Apache are after young women and horses to sell or trade. Today we have no women or horses. We should have no problem with the Apache. The Comanche," Carlos shook his head, "will kill you for anything you have. They have killed men for only a few pesos, then take their scalp."

The brothers flinched. Will was accustomed to such stories and asked, "Were you ever attacked?"

Carlos said, "Pedro and I run this route from only a few weeks ago. We haven't seen any Indians in the three runs we make." Carlos shrugged his shoulders and exhaled. "The driver and his helper before us, was killed and scalped."

Robert asked, "What happened to the passengers?"

Carlos said, "There were no survivors. I will show you, on the way to our next stop."

Sean looked worriedly at his half-brother for a moment before saying, "No, we don't want to see where it happened. Just take us back."

Carlos said, "If that's what you want—"

Will said, "Hold on there, Carlos. I must be in Los Angeles by the end of the year. I'm going on to Monterrey, with or without these two." Will wanted to get these two men back to Texas, knowing they were running away from something. His lawman instincts had taken over. Will couldn't arrest the two in Mexico or California.

After a few minutes of discussion, Will reluctantly agreed to go back. Carlos looked surprised at Will's sudden change.

Carlos said, "I will need fifteen pesos each to take you back."

Will knew all along the whole thing was a Mexican scam to fleece extra money out of them. He went along with it and said, "Worth every penny to save our scalps." Everyone agreed. Robert and Sean showed their disappointment that Will was going back with them.

Back on the mud wagon, Will told the so-called brothers that he had made it to California by land exactly eight years ago this month. He described the beautiful scenery and eating the oranges off the trees.

Sean asked, "You've been to California by land then?"

Will said, "Yes, I traveled up the Rio Grande to the Pecos, over the Rockies, and through the Mojave Desert to Los Angeles."

Robert asked, "Did you have any problems with Indians?"

Will said, "Not at all."

Sean asked, "Will, would you take us to California?"

Will said, "You will need two good horses and a trail-broke mule. That would cost you about a hundred dollars each, then grub and supplies."

Sean said, "Money is no problem to us! Can we leave soon as we get to Camargo?"

Will said, "We can't get good horses in Camargo. We'll need the best horses money can buy. I know where to get them if you have silver coin."

Robert excitedly said, "We got money." He nervously laughed as Sean gave him a hard look.

When the mud wagon arrived back at Camargo, it was dark. A few mongrel dogs barked. Someone lit a lamp in the stage office. The station master came out and spoke to Carlos in Spanish. Neither seemed surprised the passengers had returned the same day they left. Will offered Carlos ten pesos to take them across the river to the hotel.

Carlos insisted, "Ten pesos for each of you," holding out his hand.

The station master didn't sound happy, but Carlos went anyway. Will learned that Carlos owned the wagon, and he paid the station ten percent of the fare. He didn't tell them about the extras he charged the passengers to return. When they got to the ferry it was tied up for the night. Carlos untied it from its moorings. All five of them pulled the ropes that moved the small barge slowly across the river toward Davis Landing.

At the landing, Will was relieved no one else was there. He watched the suspects closely as the wagon approached the hotel. Fortunately, the lights were out and everyone was asleep. As the two men struggled to pull a large trunk off the wagon, Will pulled the gun from Sean's waist and pointed it at Robert.

Will said, "Set it down…easy." Once it was on the ground, Will said, "Carlos, get that bag with my tools of the trade."

Carlos smiled and rolled his eyes, knowing what Will was about to do.

At Will's direction, Carlos emptied the tools on the ground. Robert and Sean groaned when they saw Will's shackles and chains.

Will said, "Sit down on the ground, hands behind you."

Sean said, "Son of a bitch, I was right! You are the law." About that time, Domingo came out to see what was happening.

Will said, "Gentlemen, I'm not the law. But he is!" nodding toward Domingo. "Shackle and handcuff them, Domingo. We are taking them to Fort Ringgold."

Clay Davis came running across the street with his shotgun. "What's the commotion?" Seeing the two strangers on the ground. Clay said, "Will, you were right about these two. They are two mean bastards! Escapees from the Walls Unit over in Huntsville. They killed a guard during their escape. That one-eyed son of a bitch was fixing to be hanged. After they escaped, they headed to Galveston. Broke into the home of Robert Johnson, the county judge and postmaster of Galveston.

They killed his wife Caroline when she tried to run away. The children managed to escape. Judge Johnson was savagely beaten but will recover. What are you going to do with them?"

Will said, "Since the county still doesn't have a jail, Domingo and I are going to take them over to the fort's brig."

They walked them, single file in shackles and handcuffs. At the front gate of Fort Ringgold, two gate guards were on duty.

Will asked, "Who is your duty officer?"

The guard said, "Lieutenant Richard Russell is on duty, sir."

Will ordered, "Go get him!"

"What should I tell him?" the guard asked.

"Tell him Will Smith and the new Sheriff of Starr County have prisoners for the brig."

They waited impatiently. Lieutenant Russell finally arrived, a bit out of uniform as he was not happy to have been disturbed. "What do you need, sheriff?"

"Domingo is the sheriff; I'm just giving him a hand."

Domingo said, "These are the two criminals that escaped from the state prison recently. They broke into the home of the U.S. Postmaster in Galveston. They have committed a crime against the U.S. Government. Therefore, we are turning the prisoners over to you."

Lieutenant Russell said, "Follow me. I will need more information tomorrow. For now, they are our guests."

Back at the hotel, Alejandra had fixed Will a room. Clay Davis had told her what had occurred when they entered.

Alejandra said, "Can I fix you something to eat? I will heat you some caldo and tortillas. You will sleep good in the room I fix for you." She looked at Domingo. "And for you?"

Domingo said, "Thank you, Aunt Alejandra, nothing for me. I wish to talk to Will alone, please." Once Alejandra was in the kitchen, Domingo said, "Will, I'm glad you are back, and I hope you will stay and be our sheriff."

Will said, surprised, "Domingo, you trained hard for six weeks and I kicked your ass to get you ready for the job."

Alejandra came with the food and fresh coffee. When she left, Domingo continued, "I tried to frown at my people on the street today and they laugh at me. I can't be tough like a lawman needs to be! I discuss this with my family, and they agree. They do not want me to change, and I have no desire to be anything but who I am. Do you understand?"

Will said, "I understand, Domingo, and agree with you. What do you want to do with your life?"

Domingo said, "I want to practice law! I have received acceptance to Baylor University in Independence, Texas. I received a letter from Mr. Baylor, and he says by the time I get my degree, the Baylor School of Law will be open, and I can be in the first class."

Will said, "That sounds like a plan. You know, my father and two brothers were lawyers." Will stood. "I know whatever you do, you will be good at it. Now I need to go to bed before the roosters start to crow."

Domingo said, "Get your rest. I will see you about noon."

Will said, "That's good, Domingo."

When Will got to his new room on the ground floor, Alejandra had posted a *Do Not Disturb* sign on his door. He was glad to be home again.

Alejandra knocked on his door and said, "Will, it is time

to wake up. Someone is here to see you. They say it is very important."

Will said, "I'll be out in a few minutes." He washed his face, combed his hair, and brushed his moustache. Then called out, "I'm going to the privy."

When Will spotted the U.S. Government wagon out front, he knew it was Major LaMotte sending for him. He shut the privy door, but someone knocked on it.

Will said, "You'll have to wait your turn."

When the job was done, Will opened the door to see Clay Davis standing there. Will asked, "Don't you have your own privy?"

"Yes, I do, but I came to tell you about some good news before you go to Fort Ringgold."

Will asked, "Clay, would you please move so I can get to the washstand?"

Clay said, "Will, the one-eyed man has a thousand-dollar reward offered by the State of Texas. Judge Robertson matched it and the five-hundred-dollar reward for his accomplice. That's a total of three-thousand dollars. That's a year's wages! Aren't you excited, Will?"

Will said, "No, but I'm hungry. Let's go eat." They entered the dining room to see two corporals in army uniform.

A young corporal started to say, "Major LaMotte—"

Will said, "Yes, I know Major LaMotte wants to see me immediately! I am hungry and Alejandra has cooked my breakfast. Do you want to join me?"

The corporal said, "Well, I appreciate that, sir, as I missed breakfast on base. May the driver join us?"

Will looked at Alejandra, who nodded. Will said, "Certainly, we all have to eat."

Will arrived at Fort Ringgold headquarters to be greeted by the aide-de-camp of the base commander.

Will said, "It's good to see you again."

The aide said, "Major LaMotte has been waiting for you," as he opened the base commander's door.

Major LaMotte asked, "What's the story of the hombres you put in my brig? They told my duty sergeant you kidnapped them in Mexico."

Will grunted and said, "No, they crossed the border on the stage that I was on. They paid their fare, same as me. While getting our baggage, I discovered they were escapees from the state prison. The tall one is scheduled to be hung. The short one was serving life for his involvement in the same murder. While on the run, they broke into Robert Johnson's home in Galveston and killed his wife and beat Johnson. Fortunately, his two children escaped."

Major LaMotte said, "That's why you told the night watch to leave the shackles on." He nodded. "I can't leave the shackles and handcuffs on in my custody."

Will said, "If you take them off, have your best men unshackle them. Keep at least two guards on them night and day."

Major LaMotte asked, "How long they going to be here?"

Will said, "I will write the warden and the Galveston sheriff today. It may be a couple weeks before we know what they want us to do with them."

Major LaMotte asked, "Will, when did you decide they were outlaws?"

"The minute I laid eyes on 'em." Will stood and put on his hat.

Major LaMotte smiled and said, "That's exactly what Clay Davis told me! I'm glad you're back in Starr County."

Will replied, "Thank you, Major. It seems this is where I was meant to be."

The End

I hope you will follow the adventures of Will Smith and his friends in the next book in the Westward Sagas series.

About the Author

David A. Bowles is a fifth-generation Austinite. Both parents' families were early Travis County pioneers. His Great-grandmother, Elnora Van Cleve, is recorded as the first birth in Austin, Texas during the days of the Republic.

He named his dog Becka after Rebeckah Mitchell-Smith, his Great-great-grandmother, matriarch of the family. The author and Becka travel extensively, telling and writing the stories of the *Westward Sagas*.

David grew up listening to the stories of his ancestors told by his elders. Their stories so fascinated him that he became a professional storyteller, spinning tales through the *Westward Sagas* as well as the spoken word. He is a member of the National Story Telling Network and the Tejas Storyteller Association. David entertains groups frequently about his adventures on the open road and the books he's written.

For information on David's appearance schedule, contact holly@westwardsagas.com.

Other books by the author are available for purchase at westwardsagas.com

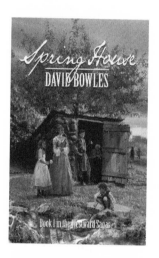

The Westward Sagas series tell the stories of the lives of Scots-Irish families struggling to find happiness on the new frontier. **Spring House** begins in North Carolina in 1762 and paints a vivid picture of colonial life in the backwoods of the Carolinas. Adam Mitchell fought to protect his family and save his farm, but his home was destroyed by British troops in the Battle of Guilford Courthouse, and his corn fields were turned into fields of death.

National Indie Excellence 2007 Book Awards announced that Spring House was a finalist in Historical Fiction category.

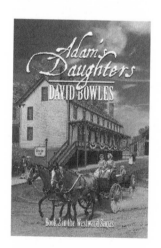

Adam's Daughters tells the story of Peggy Mitchell, a survivor of the Battle of Guilford Courthouse, who grows up in Jonesborough, Tennessee during the tumultuous first twenty years of the nation's existence. Though haunted by memories of war, she matures into a strong, independent young woman who is courted by Andrew Jackson and who has a freed slave as her best friend. Together the children of Adam and Elizabeth take on renegade Indians, highwaymen, and the hardships of an untamed land.

2010 International Book Awards finalist in the Historical Fiction category.

Ask us about purchasing the bundle directly from the author.

Children of the Revolution continues with the next generation of the Mitchell family. Peggy, the protagonist in Adam's Daughters, takes on a stronger role as she matures into a confident woman courted by British nobility.

The book uncovers the untold reason North Carolina never ratified the U.S. Constitution. Adventure, intrigue, romance, and tragedy are woven into the story of the Children of the Revolution.

2013 North Texas Book Festival finalist in Historical Fiction category.

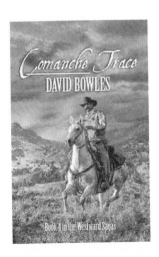

Comanche Trace is the story of Will Smith, a Texas Ranger during the early days of the Republic. His family suffers tragedy when Comanches kill Will's brother James and abduct nine-year-old nephew Fayette. Will pursues the Indians alone in hopes of rescuing the boy.

Will is caught in rifts between Texas, Mexico, and the Indians.

2020 North Texas Book Festival - First Place in Best Adult Fiction category.

Made in the USA
Columbia, SC
09 February 2023

11399351R00143